Until Death Do Us Part

"Will you let me make love to you?" he asked, his voice resonating but quiet.

She took a deep breath and nodded, closing her eyes in a futile attempt to still the furious beating of her heart. He lifted the ponytail held in place at her nape by a tortoiseshell clasp and kissed her.

Aware of her resounding heartbeats, she turned around slowly and raised her gaze to his. She read his unexpected surprise. He lifted her into his strong arms. It was easy to lose herself in those brown eyes. Yes, they were brown. They dominated his face. His irises were a captivating shade, surrounded by thick dark lashes.

She wanted him to kiss her then, but he didn't. He carried her into the deep shadows of the boathouse, where a discarded canvas tarp provided an open invitation. He laid her down on the floor and removed first his shirt, then her blouse, before covering her body with his. He was heavy, hard, and rough against her. She loved it, yet she fought the explosive desire that threatened to flood her being.

Published by
Genesis Press, Inc.
315 Third Avenue North
Columbus, Mississippi 39701

Until Death Do Us Part

ISBN 1-885478-83-6

Printed in the United States of America

FIRST EDITION

Book Design by Mary Beth Vickers

Until Death Do Us Part

Susan Paul

Genesis Press

Dedication

For Martha Hix,
my "podner" in crime,
a great romance writer,
and the best friend a gal could ever have!
I couldn't have done it without you.
Love 'choo, bébé-
Sooz

Chapter One

In her dream, it was summer and not the end of January. She ran along the dunes of Miller Beach. The fine sand of the southern island off the coast of Georgia hampered her every barefoot step. Her leg muscles burned with fatigue, yet she fled in terror, trying to escape her pursuing husband.

He called her name. "Caroline! Caroline!"

She knew if he caught her, he would suffocate her, so she ran on and on, losing more and more strength with every sinking step into the deep sand, while her husband continued to follow relentlessly. From somewhere in the distance, it seemed she could hear another man's voice. So familiar—so comforting—

Landon's voice.

She knew that if she could only let him know where she was he would save her. But she could not scream, could not make a sound. Fear had taken her voice, with Landon too far away to find her. When it seemed she could feel her pursuer's breath on the back of her very neck, she managed a faint cry and wakened herself.

Caroline, trembling, sat up in bed and wrapped the sheets about her body, clutching the smooth, cool material for reassurance. A permeating sense of panic remained after the dream, although she reminded herself again and again she was not down on the beach, was no longer married to that horrible man, but was safely in her childhood home. She was living in her recently deceased father's 1940s beach house, where she had lived before her marriage, before she and Landon had broken off their teenage love affair.

The home, poised on a rock over the Atlantic, was stately and large, the architecture celebrating the coast's sea-weathered look that had captivated her father the first time Sheldon Hunt glimpsed the house thirty years ago. Inside, downstairs, there was thick fringe on the upholstery, with a gilt mirror here, a Biedermeier chest there, all giving away that the furniture was not newly bought, but transported from a previous home. There was even a hall table that her father had fashioned from some ruins he came across one day on the beach. Always a place of great happiness and warmth. But now so painfully empty. Caroline glanced out the window from the bed. With both Mother and Father gone—with Landon as much as gone—she wondered if it would ever feel like true home again.

Caroline could hear the rushing sounds of the ocean surf, a regular rhythm not unlike the echo of her heart. It was pleasant, comforting, soothing. So why did she feel as if a sad-looking moon shone on her?

While her home stood above Miller Beach's sandy soil, she made herself take comfort in the reality of the familiar and solace in her old room in the home that seemed to grow out of the cliff like a treasured piece of driftwood.

After all, she had control of her life again, had no cause to think anything here would harm her. She was Caroline Hunt once again, and she thought of herself that way, no longer as anyone's wife.

In control, are you? Well, what about those faxes you've received at the radio station? You know they bother you more than you want to allow. What about the two predawn telephone calls, where no one spoke?

Ridiculous, worrying about piddling things like that.

Glancing at the clock, she looked past the picture of her late mother in heels and pearls—the mother who had died when Caroline was a child of seven.

The time read a quarter till eight. She had to be at the lawyer's office at nine for the reading of her father's last will and testament.

She decided to tarry a few minutes before showering and would listen to The Morning Show Crew, the team she'd just hired away from a much larger mainland station to replace Landon Shafer's Magic 97 sunrise spot.

A fact she had yet to tell him—

Flipping on the clock radio, Caroline tuned it into Magic 97's competition.

"Bright hits and smooth favorites right here. This is The Morning Crew, John and Melissa. I'm Melissa. Hope you're listening in the car on the way to work. The time is eight-oh-three. Three minutes after eight with The Morning Crew."

"This is Friday, finally. Is it going to rain this morning?"

"Well, nope."

"What's that weather look like, Melissa?"

"Partly cloudy. Chance for rain this afternoon. Eight-oh-four in the morning. Four minutes past the hour with The Morning Crew. Sixty-four degrees on the mainland. Low in the fifties tonight, with a slight chance of showers."

"Say, Melissa. Have you heard? Her name is Meredith Brooks. And, yes, her new song is...'Bitch.'"

"Na, na, na, na, na, na. I get to say bitch on the radio! You know, I can't wait, John. I'm going to tune in to Casey's Top Forty. I cannot wait to hear him say, nationwide, 'This is "Bitch."' Can you imagine it?"

"No, I can't."

"Tune in Sunday morning to hear if Casey says the word— the B word on the radio."

"Okay, back to business. We'll be talking to author Johanna Brazil this morning, later in the hour."

"That's right and she has a new release out today. You can't buy it yet, but you can win 'em here. That's right. Win 'em here before you can buy 'em."

"Johanna Brazil, the romance author? No—"

"Yes! This morning, right here, only with The Morning Crew. Romance writer, author extraordinaire, eccentric woman...hot lady...Johanna Brazil will be with us on the air."

"New book out this morning. That's right, win 'em here

before you can buy 'em. Right here, this morning. We have a special surprise. Here on the cover is—Who's this young man, this dapper young man on the cover?"

"You don't know, John? He's only the hottest, most popular male cover model in the country."

"Really?"

"You bet." Melissa chuckled. "He has long hair on this cover, but his hair is short now. Personally the long hair did something for me, but he's still very handsome."

"He does look pretty good in the artwork."

"You bet. And we're going to talk to him, too, this morning."

"Really?"

"Yes, John, direct from Hollywood, California, where he's been filming a movie. A biblical epic in which he plays a Roman soldier."

"Since he's Italian, that works well, huh?"

"Yes, it does, but he's going to talk to us first and I can't wait. He's hot!"

"Johanna's from Alma, Georgia. A local author. And we have bunches of the book here to give away, so give us a call at the station if you'd like one. Should we give away a book now, Melissa?"

"Let's do. The next caller at 555-0973 gets a free book. And, listeners, don't forget. If you have a question for Johanna Brazil, by all means, give us a call—"

"Miss Brooksie Brown is up next. Stay tuned."

The music began then. "Get up in the mornin' with the smooth and bright Mornin' Crew—"

With a chuckle and a shake of her head, Caroline moved to the edge of the bed and turned off the radio. She had definitely made the right decision by hiring John and Melissa.

Outside, the winter wind rattled the magnolia branches and the morning sun pressed at the paned glass of the attorney's office.

"Are you sure my father wanted it this way?" Caroline Hunt shifted her weight into a more comfortable position. The padding of the worn leather chair in front of Keaton Osbrook's desk was lumpy and hard. A rock would have been more comfortable.

"Yes, I'm sure," the lawyer said and ran a hand over his thick mass of slightly graying hair. "Before your father died he and I had a long discussion about how he wanted his estate divided. Although Sheldon made the provision for you to be executor of the estate and gave you sole control of the radio station, I can assure you he wanted the monies equally divided between your former stepbrother and yourself. Even so, Sheldon did stipulate that Landon Shafer must remain working at the station in order to receive any money."

Caroline twitched. She saw Landon nearly every day at the radio station. Still, the mention of him suddenly made her forget all about the hard, lumpy surface of the chair on which she sat. "That doesn't necessarily make it the right thing to do, does it? I mean the operative word here is former stepbrother, isn't it? What was my father thinking?"

Keaton eyed her speculatively and set his coffee cup aside. "Was Sheldon mentally impaired in some way that I hadn't noticed?"

Her self-confidence seeped slowly away as his gaze met hers. Quickly composing herself, Caroline leaned forward in what she hoped was an indignant pose. "All I meant was that Landon's mother and my father hadn't been married for years."

"True." Keaton ran a finger around the rim of a cracked coffee mug. "Nevertheless, it does not alter the fact that your father always thought of Shafer as his son. You know that, Caroline."

"I also know Landon is irresponsible and reckless, and has always done what he damned well pleases. His not showing up for the reading of my father's will today should make that perfectly clear."

"In his defense, he already has a certified copy."

She took a deceptively nonchalant sip of a glass of sweet tea.

"Knowing Landon as well as your father did, was precisely the reason Sheldon divided the inheritance equally, but left you as the station manager, my dear." The handsome older man chuckled.

Caroline studied Keaton's familiar gray eyes behind his wire-rimmed glasses. "You know of no other reason?"

He smiled and his head of dark curls tilted back a little. "Not that I'm at liberty to discuss."

Why should things be any different now, just because her father was no longer alive? She stood and reached across the desk to shake the attorney's hand. "Of course."

Leaving the law office, headed for her dark green Jaguar, Caroline warned herself not to get paranoid. She knew her father had always loved Landon as much as he would any son.

When he'd discovered their "temporary attraction" to each other, Sheldon Hunt had been happy. *Happy*, of all things. Her father had even acted as if he had thought they were meant to be together. How preposterous.

Then it occurred to her that it would not have been beyond her father to set the will up in just this manner to ensure—

Now that really was absurd.

Then again, she'd thought it was ridiculous when her father had warned her not to marry—

Oh, hell!

Magic 97 was housed in an old building, older even than her father's beach house, but far less attractive. Yet since childhood Caroline had loved the plainness of her father's radio station and reveled in wandering its creaky halls. Now she had inherited it equally with Landon. She knew her father had felt an even greater emotional obligation to his one-time stepson, considering that Lee Hunt had committed suicide shortly after she and Sheldon divorced.

Even now Caroline winced when she thought of the doomed woman. When her father and Landon's mother had first married, Caroline admired her a great deal, had wanted to be like her. Lee being a stunning redhead, Caroline had yearned to be rid of her own dirty-blond hair, to become flame-haired. Lee had been petite and beautiful. Caroline hated her own tall, lanky frame, with its long legs and big feet. She hated being more like Bambi than a vision of loveliness, like the cameo-faced Lee, whose eyes were not blue, or so large that her face seemed lost in them.

Yet in her childhood make-believe Caroline had been the beautiful creature, with Landon the tall, dark, and handsome hero who came to the island to sweep her off her feet and to carry her away to happily ever after.

People say young girls can't fall in love, don't have any idea what real love is. She did not believe that was true. The depth of her young love for Landon had been much more intense than any she had felt for a man since. The kiss that she would forever remember hadn't been the one she'd received from her husband on her wedding day. Landon had stolen the memorable first kiss behind a water heater while they'd been playing hide-and-seek as children. She had been nine, he ten.

Long ago Landon had cast a spell upon her, and it seemed she had never really escaped. Why couldn't she get over those days when she had thought so mistakenly that he had loved her?

His mother had died some sixteen years ago. Yet Caroline remembered—How could she not remember a woman so intensely beautiful, yet so hurtful to those who loved her? How could she ever forget, for one moment, that terrible day—

She and Landon had spent the day playing beach volleyball with friends. Caroline had been seventeen and Landon eighteen. They arrived at his mother's condominium, the place she'd bought the previous year, after her divorce from Sheldon. The teenagers assumed his mother would be home, drunk. It seemed she'd been drunk every day since breaking up with Sheldon. Both Caroline and Landon had dreaded seeing her. Yet a drunken display would have been better than the reality of finding Lee, after she had overdosed on sleeping pills.

His mother had taken the coward's way out, according to Landon. For a long time he blamed Caroline, her father, and the divorce for Lee's weakness.

Although Sheldon had taken him in, then stood by him throughout his troubled time, had sent him to college, and had loved him as a son, Landon's injury went deep.

Moreover, it seemed he had changed forever.

Stop it.

Here Caroline was lost in dark thoughts, probably an unconscious way to put off the inevitable. Never mind about his mother or the will, she must inform Landon about her decision to change his show's time slot.

She shook her head, still unable to escape the unpleasant task ahead.

Judging by the lighted sign outside studio 1A, Landon was on the air. On the other hand, perhaps he had just gone on the "hot line" and didn't want to be disturbed. For all that she knew him so well, she could never be sure of anything when it came to him.

It was not going to be a happy time, telling him why she had decided to move him from mornings to overnights.

To say Landon's ratings were not the best? An understatement. Replacing him with John and Melissa as the Magic 97 Morning Crew was in the best interest of the station as a whole. Like it or not, Landon would just have to abide by her decision.

Seeing the on-air light go off, Caroline opened the door slowly and looked into the studio where Landon sat alone. From the window a bar of amber light fell across the room. His back was to her and he didn't hear her come in. She stopped about a foot from him and said, "I'm glad I caught you."

Landon whipped around a quarter turn, caught unawares.

She looked at him and drew a deep breath. Tall, dark, and handsome as he was, he never failed to take her breath away. "We have to talk," she said.

He smiled and held up a finger to indicate he would be going on the air in a moment.

He then rifled though a stack of papers, pulled one out, and flipped on the microphone. "Your twelve in a row station, Magic 97. This is Landon Shafer and Morning Drive.

"You've gone without a new car long enough. Zero down. That's right. Zero down on the car of your choice. In-house financing. It's fast. It works. One day only, only at Sunshine Jimmy Jackson's Discount Auto Sales. The southeast coast's answer to the rising cost of car prices."

Landon flipped off the microphone to look up and see the midday disc jockey coming in. "A little early, aren't you?"

Bobbie Rae shrugged and glanced toward Caroline, who shifted her weight from one foot to the other before explaining, "I asked her to come in early. As I said before, we need to talk."

Amazement seemed to broaden his expression and straighten his spine. Standing, he towered over Caroline. "Is that so?"

"Yes. Could we go into my office?"

"Sure," he said and set down the earphones. "Looks like it's all yours, Bobbie Rae."

❦

"Dammit, Caroline. What do you mean you've hired John and Melissa for the morning spot? I work alone, you know that. How could you think I would agree to having John and Melissa on the air with me?"

"I am not putting John and Melissa on the air with you. I am putting them on the air instead of you."

His black eyebrows knit, Landon threw his hands into the air. "Are you firing me?"

"Of course not." Caroline wondered at the hope in his question. "That is, not unless you refuse to move to

9

overnights."

"Don't threaten me. I'm a good disc jockey. I can get a job anywhere."

"Ha! And frogs fly! Did you forget the proviso in my father's will? If you quit you lose your inheritance."

Anger, hot and scorching, flared in Landon's dark, dark eyes. "You can't do this."

"Oh yes, I can. Don't doubt it. If you had bothered to show up for the reading of the will, you'd know I'm telling the truth."

"I already have a copy of it. Your father's attorney mailed one to each of us last week, remember? I saw no reason to have it read to me when I can read it myself."

"Then I suggest you do so."

"Caroline, you can't be serious about moving me to overnights."

"I most certainly am."

"You can't do this. It's not right."

Caroline walked away and placed her hand on the door-knob before turning back around. "Oh, it's done and it's only good business. Now deal with it."

The moment the door closed behind Caroline, Landon Shafer clenched his fists. How could she do this to him? "Dammit to hell and back!"

He'd lost the round. So what if Caroline could force him with the restrictions of Sheldon's will? He'd think of something; he had to. He could not lose the war.

The door opened again and Landon, expecting to see Caroline, braced himself for battle. He found himself surprised to find Marita Taubold standing in the doorway with a finger pressed to her lips. He exhaled a calming breath. "What do you want?"

The receptionist immediately averted her gaze and Landon was sorry he'd snapped at her.

A drink. Generally, he didn't drink straight liquor, but three fingers of black Jack whiskey would help get his emotions under control. Somewhere in the office there would be liquor, at least there always had been, when it was Sheldon's domain, unless Caroline had tossed it out. He looked around. How could Caroline do this to him?

"What's gotten into you? Everyone at the station heard you cursing."

Landon pulled open the right bottom desk drawer and finding it empty, slammed it shut. "I should have known."

He picked up a pencil and pitched it into the trash. "Did you hear what Caroline has done now?"

"If you mean replacing you with The Morning Crew, yes. And I'm sorry."

He turned away. "Sometimes I wish I'd never met Caroline Hunt."

"Join the club," Marita said under her breath.

Landon began pacing. "I won't move to overnights. I won't do it. I won't stand by and let her ruin my career. I'll quit first."

"You can't do that, Landon."

He stopped and turned to face her. "Why the hell not?"

"Because if you quit, she wins. Is that what you want?"

"No, it's not what I want. But what else can I do?"

"You can move to overnights and make it a success." Marita shrugged. "That would show her."

"Yeah right, but how?" He pulled out a chair and plopped down.

The receptionist laced her fingers together in front of her. "Come up with a new format, something that's never been done around here, a sure winner."

"Which is?"

She came forward and placed a gentle hand on his arm. "That I don't know. You are the talent, not I, but I'm sure you will think of something."

11

When Landon Shafer left the station some time later, he was carrying a half-empty bottle of sour-mash whiskey, a bottle he'd pilfered from the program manager's bottom drawer. He tossed it in the dumpster.

Landon sighed wearily as he walked across the parking lot to his Jeep Cherokee. All he wanted was to be happy, and for Caroline to be happy. He wished her father had not died, for his sake as much as hers. She was no longer the same girl he had grown up with. He wished she had never married that bastard Wayne Nelson in the first place. He wished Sheldon had been stronger, more forceful, had stopped Caroline from marrying a man like Wayne.

Before Landon had realized it, he drove his four-wheel-drive up to a restaurant where he and Caroline used to go as teenagers. Walking through the door, he saw her. Damn her. She sat with some strange guy. Landon didn't hesitate, just walked up to her table calmly.

"I suppose this means you think you've won."

She did not respond or look up, although her companion certainly did.

Landon ignored his beady-eyed gaze. "Caroline?"

Still no response.

"Caroline Hunt!"

She put down her fork and wiped her mouth with a napkin. Placing it in her lap, she asked, "Are you speaking to me?"

"I am." Landon cleared his throat and forced himself to keep a civil tongue. "I asked a question and would appreciate a response."

"I beg to differ. You didn't ask a question. You made a statement. But, no, I do not think I've won. I merely did what I believe is best for the station."

"Really?"

"Yes, really," she said, after taking a sip of water and wiping the condensation from the bottom of the glass. "This is business, not personal. And it is obvious that you are taking this very personally."

When he moved forward to place two hands, palms down,

on the tabletop, he looked Caroline straight in the eye.

Her lunch date stood.

"I'd sit back down if I were you, buddy." Landon smiled. "'Cause I'm about two seconds away from putting a serious ass whippin' on you. And believe me I am in the mood."

Caroline's date choked, bucked, and moved, but she halted his forward motion with a touch of her hand and a shake of her head.

The room grew very quiet. Everybody stared. Finally, the waitress said, "Should I bring another chair?"

Landon shook his head. "No, I was just leaving."

Walking out the door, he heard the scuff of a chair across the old linoleum floor, with Caroline calling for him to wait.

He didn't.

And he didn't look back.

Starting the Jeep, Landon thought, Caroline was wrong about one thing. This was not about business. This was about control. She had moved him for no other reason than she had no control over her personal life.

Regardless, facts remained. He had two choices. Accept the situation and move on. Or reason with her and regain control of his show. He realized the stupidity of his second option. No one would ever take control from Caroline Hunt again. A third option surfaced. He would just have to beat her at her own game.

"Let the games begin, Caroline."

Chapter Two

Some things simply did not change. Two and three would always make five. The square would never have more than four sides. Leopards did not change their spots. And to Caroline's way of thinking, Landon would forever remain the same.

What normally should have been a sluggish Friday afternoon had turned out unsettling. After lunch, Caroline's nerves were strung tightly enough to drive a crazy person sane. She looked around and decided her office needed a face-lift. She straightened shelves and reorganized her father's files, which had never been filed correctly in the first place. It was something that needed doing for a good while; the mindless chore required little concentration and, most importantly, took her mind off more pressing issues.

Namely, her problems, her past, with Landon Shafer.

"Oh, Landon," she murmured, closing her eyes.

It had begun to rain outside and the inside atmosphere was gloomy, on par for January. In the South it rarely, if ever, snowed in winter—only rained. A perfect day for napping. Caroline grew sleepy. She curled up in the corner of the overstuffed sofa and her mind began to drift to memories.

Their first time had been pure enchantment.

She had been nervous. She'd started to leave the secluded boathouse. He stopped her. They kissed a little. She pulled back. He followed. They kissed again and again. He told her how lovely she was, how pretty her azure eyes were against the sun-kissed skin of her cheeks. He ran the pad of his thumb across the length of her mouth.

When she smiled, he said, "You have a wonderful smile. You really should wear it more often."

"Sorry. I take it out only on special occasions."

His dark head tilted forward slightly. "I'm glad you think our being together is special."

Shyly, she turned away. She stood gazing out the window, knowing she wanted something to happen, but unsure what. So she waited. Waited for him to make his move.

And he finally did.

"Will you let me make love to you?" he asked, his voice resonating but quiet.

She took a deep breath and nodded, closing her eyes in a futile attempt to still the furious beating of her heart. He lifted the ponytail held in place at her nape by a tortoiseshell clasp and kissed her.

Aware of her resounding heartbeats, she turned around slowly and raised her gaze to his. She read his unexpected surprise. He lifted her into his strong arms. It was easy to lose herself in those brown eyes. Yes, they were brown. They dominated his face. His irises were a captivating shade, surrounded by thick dark lashes.

She wanted him to kiss her then, but he didn't. He carried her into the deep shadows of the boathouse, where a discarded canvas tarp provided an open invitation. He laid her down on the floor and removed first his shirt, then her blouse, before covering her body with his. He was heavy, hard, and rough against her. She loved it, yet she fought the explosive desire that threatened to flood her being.

"Landon, this is wrong."

"Don't you think I know it?" He kissed her hungrily. Impatiently he groped for the button on his jeans. He tore his mouth free of hers. "But do you want to stop it? Can you stop it?"

His hand roved over her flesh, finding erogenous places she never before knew existed, never thought could exist. *I won't stop him,* she decided vaguely, with what mental capacity was left to her.

"We didn't plan it, did we?" she asked, lacing her arms around his wide neck and arching against him until she had molded to him as closely as their bodies would allow. "W— we didn't mean for this to happen…Oh, Landon."

They made love for the first time in the boathouse amid the smells of sand and surf and salty air and summertime, their coupling fiery and lusty. It was an awakening. He made her feel alive for the first time in her life.

Their bodies were shiny with sweat in the afterglow. Replete, they lay with limbs entwined, bits of sawgrass tangled in her hair. He playfully ruffled it, while she delighted in the way the sun shone through the old cedar shingled roof, casting strips of light and shadow on his muscular tanned chest. She thought him the most beautiful man she had ever seen, ever would see. He was not just a man. He was an angel.

It had been destined to happen, though the selection of when and where had been exclusively by chance. But when it was over, she wished it had never happened, since she knew it should never happen again, ever.

They lived in a small southern area, with strict southern values. The townspeople would not understand, nor accept, a love relationship between a stepbrother and stepsister. However legally unrelated they were, to the people of Miller Beach, she and Landon would always be siblings.

Gazing into her eyes, he must have sensed her regret. He placed his finger beneath her chin, raised her face to his, and said, "This was not a mistake. Please don't say this was a mistake. I couldn't bear it."

When the telephone rang to startle Caroline awake and out of her reflection, she nearly jumped out of her skin. Only by a sheer act of will did she manage to slow the furious beat of her heart.

She took several deep, shaky breaths before she was steady enough to reach for the receiver. "Hello."

"Caroline?"

Her hand stopped where it was on her scalp, combing hair away from her face. Her heart seemed to stop with it. *Landon.*

When he began to speak, she stopped him. She affected a business tone, saying, "Wait. Before you even start, let me ask you something."

The voice on the other end became cutting. "All right."

"Was that stunt in the Beach Café really necessary."

He hesitated for a moment. "Under the circumstances, I think so."

She exhaled. "I cannot believe you would really have started a fight, right there in front of everyone."

He made a *tsk-tsk* sound, which infuriated her.

"Caroline, Caroline. You have known me for a long time. Surely, you know me well enough to know that I don't lie. If I tell you there are blueberries on Huckleberry Hill, you know you had damned well better take your bucket with you!"

She stood and began to pace. "Are you quite finished?"

"I guess so."

"Well, I hope you're happy, because heaven knows our personal business is probably all over town by now. I'll be surprised if it's not in the newspaper tomorrow."

"You think I care?"

Caroline stopped short. "No. I do not think you care. I'm not that naïve. You have never cared about anything but yourself."

"That's bull and you know it."

She sat back down on the sofa. "What did you call for?"

"Never mind!"

The click of the telephone in her ear was considerably loud. Caroline swallowed unbidden tears, before turning her back on the radio station.

—⟡—

The rain let up on the drive home. Off in the distance the sky was clearing, Caroline could tell by the peachy glow that lit the horizon where it met the Atlantic. Above, clouds remained a dark, streaky gray. But they were in motion, lifting, dissolving in advance of a clear evening. Although it was cool, nightfall promised to turn out pretty.

She took Vermilion Street south into town, then swung over to Warren where the lighted shops and street-side parking lined both sides of the two-way boulevard that took her to Shore Drive where she made a left-hand turn at the gazebo and headed home.

She thought it strange that an ancient beige VW Bug took the same turns, but decided not to get paranoid. Besides, the tiny car turned before she reached her own street.

Caroline lived not too far down the road and directly across from the Atlantic's rocky shore. She steered the Jaguar up the winding white shell drive leading between the line of ancient live oaks, which draped their traditional streamers of Spanish moss and lined the drive almost up to the beach house.

Slowing the car, she reached out the window and touched a streamer of dry gray moss with her fingers, remembering old times, happy times. She remembered when her mother had called it witch's hair, and sometimes used strands of it beneath a pointed cap as part of Halloween costume she'd created. But only after her mother had made certain all the red bugs had met their demise. Thank goodness.

When Caroline stopped the car, she glanced up at the house. As always, her family home had the power to move her deeply, though its sheer beauty was breathtaking in a way she could not help. To Caroline, the Hunt beach house bespoke the most beautiful clichés of Southern summer homes. Such homes were not typical of the island, but she would forever be grateful to the person who had built this residence, for not choosing the more usual plantation house.

A stepping-stone walk led to the rear entrance and was hooded by a white wooden arbor, entwined with wisteria just outside the kitchen door. She passed beneath it on her way to the door, glancing at the twisting bare limbs, imagining how beautiful the flowers would look come spring with their purple and white blooms.

Beyond the large azalea bushes that surrounded the house, those flowers were all that was left of her mother's garden. Caroline carefully took care of the wisterias, pruning and watering them all through the long, hot summer months.

She stepped into the kitchen and was greeted by Sandy Prator, a slightly graying, dark-haired, petite woman, who had not only been her housekeeper, but also her best friend for the past year. Though not classically pretty, Sandy definitely had her points. Her skin was fair with a sprinkling of freckles across her nose—almost as if she had been meant to be a redhead. Her green eyes tilted up slightly at the corners and were framed by brows and lashes so dark they made the irises seem even greener. Unfortunately she absolutely refused to wear makeup and thereby failed to make the most of her appearance.

"Well, hey there, Caroline. Home a bit early, ain't cha?"

"Yes, I guess I am."

"C'mon over here an sit with me for a bit. Hope you're not too hungry, 'cause supper's still 'bout thirty minutes off."

"No, Sandy, I'm not hungry," she replied taking off her coat and sitting at the kitchen table. "Not in the least bit. Take your time."

Sandy stirred Brunswick stew on the stove and tapped the wooden spoon against the side of the pot. "Bad day at Black Rock, I take it?"

"You could say that and then some. It wasn't pleasant."

Leaving the stove to pour Caroline a glass of sweet tea, Sandy said, "You told Landon you've replaced him and he was not happy."

Caroline took the tall glass with hand-painted pheasants on the sides and raised it in a mock salute. "Bingo. You know, Sandy, sometimes I wish his mother had drowned him at birth."

Sandy handed her a small bowl of sliced lemon and retied her gingham apron. "Why am I not surprised?"

Caroline shrugged, squeezed some lemon into her tea, stirred, then took a good swallow.

"I agree Landon may not be a perfect man, but he surely is little bit of heaven right here on earth," Sandy remarked.

Caroline choked and barely kept from sending a good-size stream of tea out her nostrils. "W—what do you mean by that?"

"I mean…that man is altogether yummy."

Some thirty minutes later, Caroline told Sandy to forget about supper and go on home. Opening the door, the house-keeper turned to look back, saying, "The stew's in that blue plastic bowl in the fridge. I want you to promise you'll eat some of it before you go to bed."

Caroline, unsmiling, looked up from the Times. "I promise," she said quietly, then added, "Promise you will stay for dinner tomorrow night and help me finish it off."

"Promise."

"And don't forget to lock your car doors and be careful on the way home."

Sandy giggled. "In a town the size of Miller Beach, I hardly think there is any need to lock my doors for the mile and a half drive home."

"You know what kind of world we live in. You read the newspapers. Now, just be careful."

"All right. I will."

An intimate silence hung between the two friends for a moment before the door closed.

In bed watching a video, eating buttered popcorn and drinking cola, Caroline noted that the Sophia of the film didn't have any more of a clue to life than she did, but the film character wasn't bewildered by the fact. After her divorce, Sophia picked herself up and started all over again without ever looking back. "Here's my number. Call me sometime," she said to the handsome stranger she had just met.

Caroline continued to watch the movie instead of sleeping. Sophia found the career she had always wanted and the love of her life.

Sophia remarried, had a child.

Sophia lived happily ever after.

It was just a story after all, real life.

In real life, Caroline watched a movie in her bed on the island. She was alone in the world. She had great career. But she did not have a man who loved her more than life itself, or a child.

One o'clock in the morning and still unable to sleep, Caroline got out of bed and pulled on her thick terry robe and old slippers. Taking a large flashlight from her bedside drawer, she headed down the winding staircase, through the hall and out the door.

Moonlight dappled the high branches of live oaks and magnolias. Thousands of bright stars covered the clear night sky. The cool, crisp air stung her face causing her to shiver and pull her robe more tightly about her, seeking its comforting warmth.

She walked between the tall sawgrass, lost in fanciful thought in spite of herself. As she headed down toward the beach, she felt a sense of nostalgia that she tried vainly to stifle. The full sense of the island enveloped her, seduced her. As a young girl, this was a frightening spell, one she did not understand. She reminded herself mockingly of those foolish days of childhood.

There were no marshes close to Miller Beach, but the smell of it pervaded the island, that damp, slightly tangy odor of wet grasses and mucky soil running alongside the river. Gentle sea breezes blew, bringing with them a faint fishy smell. She quickened her steps, glancing about carefully beneath the full moon's light, watching for the bend in the path that led down to the boathouse. Waves lapped at the shore in a familiar rhythm and the roar of the ocean filled the night.

With the flashlight's wide beam of light, she searched the

21

sandy dunes ahead of her. There it was, the turn. And the old boathouse came into sight, a small weathered building now in need of repair.

As Caroline studied the place more closely, her stomach dropped. The structure evidently had not been painted in a decade. Not by anything except seagull droppings. Even by only the flashlight beam and the shining moon, she could see that. Why had she not noticed before the boathouse's sad state of disrepair? Because I avoided coming down here, that's why. So why in the world am I here now?

Devil if she knew.

She marched up to the door and opened it. A beady-eyed stray dog jumped up from where he had been sleeping on the floor and howled at her. She came up short and set her teeth to keep from screaming.

"Get," she yelled. "Get your mangy, Heinz 57-looking butt out of my boathouse!"

Fortunately for the dog, he seemed to take her seriously and went on his way without so much as a bark of retaliation.

Caroline stepped over the threshold and went inside. With one hand on her hip and the other controlling her flashlight she looked around dubiously. The floorboards had holes in them where feet had gone right through.

She picked her way across the good boards to the wall. Wonder of wonders, it still had electricity, although the bare single bulb hung more than a little askew in its socket. There was sand and dead sawgrass and bits of driftwood everywhere. The floorboards were littered with it.

"Time certainly has a way of unromanticizing things," she announced, speaking to no one and looking for God.

But there it was. She could still make out the old carving on the wall. She reached out, touched it with her fingers, tracing the space where the wood had been chipped away, where crude lettering had been carved into the panel. She touched the top line and then moved below. LANDON, the bottom letters spelled. He'd carved it after they made love that long-ago midsummer's day. Then she had taken the Swiss Army knife and etched her name above his, although she'd protested that her name ought to be below his. Landon said no, it belonged above. After all, she was a Hunt and this was her father's boathouse, not his. His, too, she'd pointed out, although he had come here only because his mother had married her father.

So the names had stayed over the years, still marking the boathouse and giving evidence of the young lovers they had once been, offering proof of their mistake.

Caroline knew she needed to forget about all this. That was what her mind said. She just wished somebody would explain it to her heart.

Chapter Three

Monday morning. How he hated Mondays. Especially this Monday.

Landon had intended to haul it out of bed early, despite the fact he did not have to go on the air until midnight. But his intentions weren't strong enough to do the job and it was after twelve before he rolled over groggily and rubbed the sleep from his eyes. He yawned and stretched, cutting the motion short when he glimpsed the copy of the legal document on the bedside table.

Easing gingerly to his feet, he decided his headache wasn't nearly as bad as he feared it would be, but the hangover made up for it.

Still bitter and furious, Landon choked back bile. What could he do about the way the will had been drawn up now? He probably couldn't do anything about it, even if Sheldon Hunt were still alive. The old man would only say it was his business and his decision, considering that he didn't have to leave Landon anything at all. They weren't even related. Landon was nothing more than a former stepson. There was nothing he could do about the will. Nothing he could do about anything. Not a damn thing.

Except—

Landon jumped out of bed and snatched the blue-backed document from the night table. He marched to the other side of the bedroom and tossed Sheldon Hunt's last wishes in the garbage.

Okay, so he might not know who said, "All's fair in love

and war," but, by damn, Landon would take him at his word!

He gathered up his clothes, then beat a path to the bath-room.

—⟡—

Out of the shower Landon felt considerably better, although still in need of some aspirin and a strong cup of coffee. He turned on the water in the kitchen sink, made the coffee, then reached for the cabinet door above the stove and retrieved a bottle of aspirin. After popping two pills, he washed them down with a swig of tap water.

Leaning against the counter, he had no doubt Caroline was simply angry at the world and therefore being unreasonable. The overnight shift at a radio station being nothing more than a last stop, he knew it was a place where washed-up deejays went to die. And Caroline knew it, too.

Admittedly, his ratings had fallen lately, but that didn't mean he couldn't get them back up. He would just have a talk with Caroline again and convince her that this time, they could come up with a viable solution together.

On the third ring, she picked up the telephone.

"This is Landon."

"Okay."

"Caroline?"

"What do you want?"

"I want to talk to you."

"So talk."

Two times, he paced the length of the crescent-shaped kitchen counter. Why was she always so damned angry?

"Caroline, I have no desire to go to overnights and you know it. I know you're upset about your father's death and so am I, that goes without saying. But we need to set everything aside, so we can come up with a solution to our problems."

"First, let me assure you this has nothing to do with my father." Her voice on the other end of the line got colder, if possible. "Second, we don't have any problems. You have the

25

problem. You don't want to accept my decision to replace you with John and Melissa in the morning."

"I can't accept your decision."

"You have no choice."

"Oh, yes I do. I can quit."

"Yes, you can do that. I didn't realize you cared so little about money."

"What do you mean by that?" he asked.

"Simply, you know my father's will states that if you quit, you lose your inheritance. Are you telling me you're willing to give it up?"

He didn't say a word.

"I didn't think so," she said. "As I said before, you can move to overnights or you can quit. It matters little to me either way. So what's it going to be?"

"I promise you, Caroline, I'll prove you've made the wrong decision. And I will be back on Morning Drive."

"Famous last words."

He could just imagine her big blue eyes crinkling at the corners.

She went on, "I'll expect you on the air tonight at midnight with an entirely new format for your show."

He didn't argue with her. It would have been futile, but he was not beaten yet. He would just have to think of something.

But what?

—⟨⟩—

At three o'clock that afternoon Landon walked into the radio station where the day had just begun to wind down. Marita the receptionist, obviously glad to see him, sat at her desk with a smile on her face, waiting for him to approach her.

Even before he had a chance to get there, she came forward to meet him halfway. Landon felt no rush of emotion at the sight of Marita Taubold rising, pretty, petite, and smiling, from the chair. But it swept down upon him with a force he had not expected, when he found himself unconsciously assessing the qualities of her beauty as compared to Caroline Hunt's. *Geez, I've lost my ever-lovin' mind.*

"Good afternoon, Landon."

"Hi." It took an effort to speak when he was this aggravated with himself. "The day going all right for you?"

"Much better, now that you're here."

"Well, thanks." He met her smile, before leaving the reception area.

He headed straight for his office at the back of the station, passing Caroline's doorway. The thought of her presence behind that closed door gave him a jolt not unlike the ones he'd experienced as a teenager, when he had a crush on her and would walk down the hallway past her room to the bathroom more times than necessary during a day. But the jolt this time had nothing to do with crushes. It had to do with the feeling of being cheated out of something that was not rightfully his in the first place. And about the uncertainty of his feeling for Caroline, and how to handle the situation at hand.

Landon went into his office and closed the door, sitting down with a breath that puffed out his cheeks. He sat for a minute wondering what to do next. The picture of the two of them when they were teenagers kept playing inside his head. He wondered, *Would we be together now if either of us had defied convention and not cared what anyone else thought? And will I ever get over her?*

For the duration of a sigh he let his eyes close and his shoulders curl backward against the chair. When the heater started to blow he jumped. Sitting straighter, he made a decision. He would create a show format that could not possibly be anything but successful.

He quickly dialed Keaton Osbrook's office to make certain he stood within his rights. Ten minutes later, Landon had been assured that he was.

With a chuckle he pulled open the drawer and extracted a notepad and tore off the top sheet. He set out to outline his idea for the new show.

—◄※◆※►—

At eight o'clock that evening Landon parked his Jeep Cherokee at the bottom of the drive and got out slowly. The driveway climbed at a steep angle. Pausing with his hand on the door, he studied the beach house that hadn't changed since he had lived there with his mother and Sheldon...and with Caroline. The home was still as impressive as ever: two-story with a garage for three cars, built on a rock overlooking the Atlantic.

The garden would not bloom again until spring, but he had no trouble imagining what it would look like then—as beautiful as Caroline herself.

He slammed the Jeep's door and approached the house with his every instinct urging him to return to the station, to let her find out about his show when she heard him on the air at midnight.

But he could not.

He rang the doorbell instead, waiting with his key ring caught over his index finger, dreading the moment when she opened the door, realizing that within the next few hours he was going to change the way things had always been done at Magic 97. Forever.

Caroline opened the door and stared at Landon in stunned surprise. Dressed in loose-fitting white silk lounging pajamas with no bra, she stood barefoot. Her face had been scrubbed clean of makeup, her hair pulled back in a loose ponytail at the back of her slender neck.

"Hello, Caroline," he said at last.

She clutched her chest as if self-conscious. "Why are you here?"

"I thought we should talk before I go on the air tonight." He kept the keys handy in case she slammed the door in his face. Blocking his entrance, she looked less than pleased by his presence. She moved not a muscle, her face devoid of anything resembling a welcome.

"Don't you think we should discuss the format for my

show tonight before you hear it on air?" he challenged.

She released a breath and stepped back. "I suppose we should."

Certain that he smelled the scent of spiced pears, he stepped inside, entering the foyer that segued into the vast combination living room/dining room. The room, which soared to a twenty-foot ceiling, was even more beautiful than before, since the west wall, once redwood, had been white-washed. Caroline had also replaced the old furniture with a chunky stuffed chaise and sofa with pale blue print cushions, and a weighty iron Gothic coffee table topped with yellow daffodils. It was as if a patina of time ran through the house, seasoned by many years of beachside living.

"Sit down, so that we can get this over with," she said, moving past the wide picture window that faced the ocean, stopping near the stairway.

He stood in front of the off-white chair and waited. She moved around the back of the sofa and took a seat, leaving plenty of room between them. When she sat, he did the same.

Tension pervaded the room. He felt himself struggling to frame the correct words, to suppress his nervousness about being alone with her again after all these years. Many times they had been together with others at the station but never just the two of them. Caroline, it appeared, had her mind made up to fix her gaze on the Atlantic and leave it there.

He leaned forward with elbows on his knees, his hands clasped in front of him. "I'm going to do a kind of sex therapy call-in show. I heard a station in Seattle doing a similar type of show when I was out there on vacation last summer."

"What? Have you lost your mind?" Caroline shot to a standing position and waved a hand erratically. "No, Landon, out of the question."

He raised a hand like a stop sign. "Before you go and take a giant leap for morality on me, just hear me out."

With balled fists on hips, she raised one golden eyebrow in his direction. "I am not about to let you sabotage my female demographic listeners. You know we're in the South! These are conservative people here, we are not on the West Coast."

Tired of having to look up at her, he stood and slipped his hands into his pockets. "I don't think that will be a factor. The Southern Bible Beaters Convention will all be in bed. Besides, the callers will be females, ages twenty-five to forty. That is the station's format demographic, isn't it?"

"I think you will offend more people than you'll have participating."

"It is in the overnights, Caroline. It is not as if children will be listening," he said on a sigh.

She moved forward then and shoved a fingertip soundly against his chest. "You think I'm a fool? You think I don't know this is nothing more than your way of driving the listeners away, so that John and Melissa do poorly in the ratings?"

Landon turned his back to her and ran a hand through his hair. "Oh, yeah right. Like I want the station's numbers to suffer. I still work there, you know."

"What about our advertisers? Most of them are religious conservatives. They'll go off the deep end when they hear about this."

He turned around to face her. "I personally think for every advertiser we lose, we'll gain two in their place. The ratings will rise with this type of show."

"I don't agree."

"Caroline, think about it. Women will call in with their problems and other women will have helpful solutions and/or similar stories. Dammit! It's a no-lose scenario!"

She shook her head. "Sorry, Landon. You will not do this."

"I won't?" he challenged.

"Don't push me. The only reason you got a job in radio in the first place was because my father owned the station. No one else in their right mind would have hired you, much less kept you on the air when your ratings took a nosedive. If you try to put a live sex-fantasy format on the air, I swear, I will terminate you."

"Really? I'd check your father's will, if I were you, before making so bold a statement. If you force me off the air, you will lose your inheritance."

"That can't be."

"Believe me, it can."

Chapter Four

Caroline glared at the door Landon had just slammed behind him. Fury heated her cheeks—how easily he'd made her make a fool of herself. She rolled her lips inward to keep from uttering the swear words that surged to her tongue. Why, the way she felt, she'd find and murder him, if it wasn't so damned hard to get blood out of silk lounging pajamas!

Taking hold of her self-control, she made it to her bedroom to lie down on the bed and gather her wits. Flinging an arm over her eyes, she thought, *Heavens, but I feel drained.*

Her four limbs seemed to weigh a ton apiece. Five minutes later, a few minutes after ten, she heaved a heavy sigh and swung her feet to the floor, to sit on the edge of the bed. Then she snapped her fingers.

Reaching in the drawer of the bedside table, she pulled out her father's will and held it against her chest, pretending her breasts weren't flushed with heat. She flipped through the pages, searching for an answer to her problem. There was none. At least, none that she could determine. As much as she hated to admit it, it looked as if Landon was right. If she fired him, she would lose her inheritance. What on earth could her father have been thinking?

According to the stipulations, Landon could do as he pleased on his show as long as it was within FCC regulations. And there was not a single thing she could do to stop him. She stood, trying to pretend her legs weren't wobbly and weak.

Damn, damn, and double damn!

On the way out, she sailed her copy of the will on top of the dresser.

She slammed her bedroom door with violent temper; not in more than a year had she been so consumed with white-hot rage. Although time had passed, dark memories surfaced of the last time that matters had been wholly beyond her control.

Although most of the pain had receded, there were moments, like this one, when it came rushing back, taking her by surprise with its intensity. She tried to squash the bad memories but they seemed determined to linger.

She would never forget that gloomy, rainy afternoon of her last fury.

"You cannot be serious," she'd said, troubled and uncertain. Disbelieving.

Wayne Nelson's face had been calm, his manner assured. "I am indeed. You would never have had a miscarriage if you'd stayed home and not insisted on continuing to work. I'm sorry, but if you want us to try once again to have a child, then you must give up working and concentrate on family."

This was not what she wanted. She sought a miracle, according to Wayne, yet had no right to ask. She wanted, somehow, to have a child and to keep her career.

She shivered and went to look out at the rain, where it beat a wedding-quilt design across the puddle in the road. "Losing the baby had nothing to do with work. Pregnant women work all the time," she said. "The miscarriage was something that just happened, something beyond anyone's control but God's."

Her husband moved to stand beside her at the rain-streaked window, but he did not place his arm around her in any attempt at comfort.

"So you'd rather risk losing another baby, than give up your career in radio," he said.

No, that was not true. She knew it wasn't. Her doctor had said the miscarriage wasn't any fault of hers; Wayne knew that. But maybe she was being selfish. She did want a baby and a career, something for herself. Was that so terribly wrong? No, she didn't believe so. She had given and given to Wayne, so why couldn't she have the right to keep on living?

"I would not put any child of mine in harm's way intentionally," she said. "But I do not want to stay home all the time, either. I want to work. Do you really think it would be better if I gave up my career, had a child, and was then unhappy staying at home?"

"You're simply not being fair."

"You keep telling me I'm not fair to you, but life's too short, Wayne. Every woman needs something of her own."

He was silent for a few moments, before backing away from her. "If this is truly how you feel, you're not the type of woman I want to be married to. I think it would be best if we started divorce proceedings."

A divorce?

It wasn't as if she had devoted all her time to her job during their marriage. She lavished her attention on everything from the shiny hardwood floors in their newly renovated Victorian to the new coat of paint on the cabinets and the cabbage rose-flowered wallpaper. She had made their house a home, made it warm and inviting.

She had given Wayne her love.

What had he offered her in return? Had he made her happy as he'd promised he would do the day they exchanged vows? Not even when he made love to her. Not when he had doubted himself and she made him believe there was nothing he couldn't do.

"Did you hear me, Caroline? It's your job or a divorce. Take your pick."

All of her dreams melted like sugar in the rain that day of their breakup. Wayne Nelson destroyed her just as surely as if he had stabbed her with a knife, but he had started trying to destroy her soul, from the very day they were married. She simply hadn't recognized it.

A few months later, she was not only childless, she was also divorced and living at her father's home again. Her now ex-husband had left for a new job and a new life in Chicago. Her heart had been shattered, but he apparently made the transition well.

If she had it to do all over again, she would have done things differently. Oh, yes, she would. She would have listened to her father and never married Wayne. Sheldon Hunt had been right. Wayne hadn't been the man for her. Not at all. She'd been a lonely fool, thinking he loved her.

Now there was a wall between her and her heart. She would not allow her heart to break again. And her life would not come to a standstill over anything to do with a man. She was no longer a naive wife without a clue how to take control of her life, or how to handle her own emotions. She was an independent woman, an executive.

And now Landon Shafer was encroaching on her territory.

A sex-fantasy call-in show indeed! Was that how he thought he would control her and get his show back on the Morning Drive? Maybe Landon thought control of the station should be his, too; maybe he considered himself so valuable to the station that there was no way she could get rid of him. If so, he'd soon find out she was the boss at Magic 97. She was in charge!

He signed on at exactly midnight.

"This is Magic 97. I'm Landon Shafer, your host for 'Sinful Secrets,' a new show on the air after midnight. Hosted by adults, for adults, right here on the dial. Pick up the phone, 555-FANTASY, to share your most sinful secret or sexual fantasy. That number again, 555-FANTASY."

Landon turned off the microphone and looked at his producer behind the glass. "Any calls coming in, Mike?"

"No, man. Not a one."

Landon shoved his hand through his hair. "Dammit! My butt is on the line here with Caroline."

"Don't know what to tell you. Looks like you'll just have to straight jock it until a call comes in. Don't know what else you can do."

"Hope we get a caller soon." Landon fidgeted in his seat.

"If we have to play music for more than ten minutes straight, this show is going to be history."

The white clock on the wall with large black numbers read, seven minutes and counting. Landon began to sweat.

Finally, Mike tapped on the glass. "We've got a lady on line one. She won't give her name—"

Landon released an expansive breath and slipped on his headphones. "That's okay. Throw it to me right after this song."

"You got it!"

Thirty seconds later the On-Air light illuminated above Landon's door and Mike held up a hand. He signed with his fingers—three, two, one—then pointed to him and mouthed, "You're on."

Landon took a deep breath.

"Magic 97 and 'Sinful Secrets.' Your chance to share your utmost sexual fantasies every weeknight from midnight till two. The number to call is 555-FANTASY, and we've got our first caller. Hi, you're on the air."

Dead air.

"Hi, you're on the air with Landon Shafer and 'Sinful Secrets.'"

Still, no response. Landon looked to Mike for help, but he only shrugged.

Some producer, he thought. "Caller, are you there?" If his butt was going to be saved, he was going to have to do it himself.

"Um, y—yes—I—"

Yes, Landon thought. *There is a God.* "Don't be nervous, you don't have to give your name."

"Okay."

For some reason the female voice on the other end of the wire sounded familiar, but Landon couldn't place it. He was probably just imagining things.

"Just pick a name, any name," he suggested.

"All right. How about Kitten?"

"You got it, Kitten. Listeners, if you've just tuned in, we

are on the air with Kitten. Kitten, are you still on the line?"

"Yes, I'm here."

"All right, Kitten. What's your fantasy or sinful secret that you would like to share with us?"

"Nine to five."

"Would you care to elaborate?"

"Nine to five. He's the horny boss and I'm the unsuspecting, demure secretary."

"Sounds interesting. Have you ever acted this fantasy out?"

"Not yet, but I am planning to very soon."

"Really?"

"Oh, yes."

"Does this boss have a clue?"

"Not yet, but I am sure he'll catch on real quickly."

Landon raised an eyebrow at Mike. "I guess he would. Kitten, do you think you will get what you want out of this?"

"Oh, most definitely. I'm not the type of woman who takes no for an answer, if you know what I mean."

Landon adjusted his seat in the chair. "Then—you always get what you want?"

"Let's just say I've never had a man turn me down yet."

"Kitten, thanks for calling in."

"You're very welcome. Maybe I'll come up and see you sometime."

The line went dead.

Landon did not miss a beat. "Listeners, was that woman too hot to handle, or what? Fantasizing—What does it mean? What is the deeper significance? Do our desires signal deep neurosis. Do our sinful secrets reveal suppressed feelings? Possibly, probably, and so what? There is a time and a place for deep psychological analysis, but this show is not it. No therapist here. Your tuned into 'Sinful Secrets', your sexual fantasy show. Telephone 555-FANTASY to reach Magic 97."

Landon snatched off his headphones and turned to face Mike in the booth. "That was the hottest woman I've ever talked to."

Mike nodded. "I wonder what she looks like."

"If she's as hot as that fantasy, I'd guess centerfold material."

"More than likely, she resembles my Aunt Aida. You know, the one that's so fat that if she sat on a rainbow, Skittles would pop out?"

Landon laughed. "No doubt. How are those calls looking now?"

"All ten lines are steady, man."

"Yes! Hey Mike, throw me another caller right after this commercial set."

"You got it, buddy. You're the man."

—⊰◈⊱—

At one twenty-five A.M., after forcing herself to listen to several more callers, Caroline flipped off the radio then jerked the covers under her chin. One "fantasy caller" was more than enough for her. She was going to sleep!

As she dozed off, she felt a strange, sudden need for comfort, a yearning to be nearer to Landon's hard body. Dreaming, she snuggled up against him.

A faint masculine perfume rose from his warm skin, the type of skin only men had, not soft like a woman's, but silky nonetheless.

She raised her chin, and slanted him a look from under her lashes. "Landon?"

He gave her an odd sidelong glance. "What?"

He was standing near an outdoor elevator, his hair mussed, his face moist and flushed, his thick dark-lashed eyes infinitely beautiful by sunlight. And he stared at her. Again, she thought how handsome he really was, his body was. He had the body every man should have, including the square jaw with a cleft chin. Her lips parted as if she might say something but no words came forth. She was magnetized by him; she wanted to touch his skin, his hair, and she found herself remembering, quite abruptly, their one and only sexual encounter, the first one she had ever experienced.

It was exhilarating to feel that way again. She shivered a little and felt goose bumps rise on her arms. The way he was looking at her—she felt strange. No, what she felt was excited. Sexually. And she was unprepared for the blast of heat, the physical takeover of mind and body. Then she felt a flush of wet heat between her thighs, which caused her to squirm. Instantly she tried to put it out of her thoughts, but they were not about to go anywhere.

Landon watched her closely as he pushed the elevator button. She wondered if he could sense the feelings that were permeating her, were coursing through her limbs?

It hardly seemed possible. Yet she knew it was there, hot and moist between her legs. Physical evidence she could not ignore. She had never felt more aroused in her life and she wanted—no, she needed release.

Caroline blinked, better judgment rearing. She couldn't accept what was happening. Yet—neither could she rebel against it. What would be wrong with—?

Boldly, uncharacteristically, she slipped her hand between Landon's hard muscled thighs and kneaded his resting shaft to attention.

He momentarily closed his eyes and sucked in a quick breath. "What's this?"

She smiled at the obvious pleasure she brought him and continued her ministrations. He tensed all over. That she could so easily do that to him gave her a sense of power.

She watched his lips compress and his black brows draw together above the darkest of brown eyes; she could feel her nipples burning against her blouse, the thin cotton panel of her panties soaking wet against her skin.

She reached up and held his chin, studying his face, kissing him on the cheek. "Thank you for not leaving the station. I owe you."

The elevator roared to a stop, the sliding doors parting. She felt his hand on her wrist.

"I'm very glad to hear it," he murmured huskily, "but what

39

I want to know is when can I expect payment?"

Caroline had not anticipated him saying that. She hadn't thought beyond the moment. But she did now, and thought, *Why not?*

"When do you want it?" she countered seductively.

Suddenly Landon was the one smiling. "Now would be as good a time as any."

Before she had time to think, he took a firm grasp on her elbow and ushered her into the elevator.

As the double doors moved together with a sucking noise, Landon said nothing, only reached in front of her and pushed the button for the upper floor. The elevator made a loud grinding noise. And with a rumble of protest that attested to its advanced age, the machine jerked into motion.

The movement was so abrupt Caroline almost lost her balance. Although it was not necessary, Landon instinctively reached out to steady her with a strong hand. Three seconds later, caught between floors, the elevator lurched to a halt.

Her gaze flew to his. "This is just great."

"I think it's perfect."

Landon pulled her to him. She sucked in a breath, then swallowed hard, as he said, "I meant it when I said now was as good a time as any."

"We're in an elevator—with a room full of people waiting for us in my office. You're not serious."

He didn't so much as blink. "Serious as a heart attack."

No, he couldn't be.

She tried to push him back. "L—let go of me. You've lost your mind."

His mouth came down on hers hard. It was a fiery, possessive, savage kiss that enraged her. How dare he? He had no right. She could give him anything she liked, but he could not just take it. She wouldn't let him.

Instinct took over. With lightning speed she raised both arms between his, knocking his arms away, and gave him a mighty shove with a forearm. But the attempt to distance herself from him failed.

He would not budge. Nor would he be denied. Fear of falling under his spell forever—at least she thought it was fear—once again consumed her. Her breathing quickened; her heart rate accelerated. She tore her lips away, and tried to avert her head.

Landon jerked his thickly muscled neck free, snatched her hair free of its ponytail, and shoved both hands deep into the thick waves and held her head in a helpless, immovable, captive state between his strong hands.

"You started this. Finish it."

Caroline's mouth dropped open; she was trembling. He thrust his tongue into her mouth swiftly and surely. It was an invasion, pure and simple, but not a cruel one. Still, the violation was so absolute, so irrevocable, that it was shocking in intensity. She was on the brink of being violated, and she wanted to be.

Landon closed all ten fingers in her hair and pulled her head back, forcing her to look up at him.

"Kiss me back."

Caroline's fingers dug into his shoulders but barely dented the solid muscles beneath. She stared at him with wide-eyed apprehension as he forced her against the wall of the elevator. His entire lower body was rock-hard as he pressed into her softness. There was no escape if he did not want her to go, she knew that, but what was more frightening than his control over her physically was her reaction to him.

Fear made her hot. The desire burnt to an ache inside her. She moaned softly, a wildfire sensation radiated through her, and she squeezed his shoulders.

"S—someone will come—"

"Yeah, and it's gonna be you."

"Landon!"

"Shhh." A smile crinkled his tanned face and then his lips were against her cheek. "It will take somebody a considerable amount of time to figure out what caused the elevator to stall."

Landon released his grip on her hair and held her head in both his hands. He touched her cheek; he leaned his face toward her, pressed his forehead against hers. She made a small uncertain movement, and this time the kiss he gave was again open-mouthed. But it was a wet, slow taking, over and over, and she went limp against him, moaning out loud and she knew this joining would even be better than their first.

She melted at his tenderness. It seemed her sex was growing impossibly hot, full. She felt him unbutton her blouse and expose her breasts. He pressed the sides, accentuating the deep cleavage as he sidled closer and rubbed himself against her. Then he ran the rough palms of his hand seductively over her nipples, arousing them.

Caroline's eyes became hooded, her well-kissed lips dropped open with lascivious expectation as he pressed his knee between her legs and lifted it against her.

"I—I take it you've done this before," she whispered.

Landon gripped her hips with both hands, moved his seductive gaze to hers, and cocked one dark eyebrow.

"You don't remember?" he asked, low and lusty, manipulating her pelvis.

Her breath caught in her throat. "I—I meant...in an elevator."

"Can't say that I have. Until now."

He ground against her for a moment, then his hands were loosening the tightness around her waist, breaking open the fly of her jeans faster than she could have done herself.

He pulled the jeans down and lifted her out of them. The next thing Caroline knew she was bare from the waist down and he knelt on his knees before her, spreading her legs wide apart with his hands and looking at her sex. And this time she didn't resist.

When he touched the thick thatch of blond hair with his mouth, she sucked in her breath.

"You are beautiful," he said. "The way you are breathing and moving, the hair glistening, the pink lips quivering. I want to taste you, have you like this, put my tongue inside you."

"You can't, I can't do this," she said. "It's too, it's too—"

He had his shirt open in a second. She heard the sound of

loosening fabric as he pulled it off his shoulders until it hung from his waist, as he opened his pants and freed his already hard member, all the while nibbling at the tender skin on the inside of her thighs, in the crease of her legs, around the triangle of moist down. Her legs trembled and threatened to buckle, but one large hand steadied her while the fingertips of his other hand caressed her slick folds, prolonging the anticipation of pleasures yet to come.

Suddenly the heat inside her body became suffocating and she jerked her shirt all the way off. He lifted the hand that had been supporting her and grasped her aching breast. It was hot, the nipple like a gumdrop. As he caressed it, she moaned.

She watched as he slowly brought his hand to his mouth to wet his finger with saliva. She throbbed heavily, moisture flowed, and increased her heat; her hips gyrated. He lifted one of her bare feet and placed it on his strong shoulder. He touched her lightly, hesitantly at first and a burst of pleasure so intense ran though her lower extremities that she pulled away from him.

For a moment he indulged her whim and left his fingers posed just inches above the now swollen lower lips. His hard length increased sizably, and she didn't want it to stop, not yet. She wanted to linger, relishing the slow torturous, needful, pleasurable pain this man pulled from her at the sight of him naked and wanton before him.

He expertly parted her moist folds; he blew cool air on her heated flesh; she moaned softly, the only response she was capable of, knowing they were in a public place and doing very private things.

Not caring, she grasped his neck and laced her fingers in the dark locks that curled at his nape. Mindlessly she pulled him to her. Then he was nipping her and kissing her, and diving his tongue into her, licking at the silky hair, and she was going crazy.

Then he stopped.

She clawed at him. "Don't stop."

He slipped a finger inside her. Her heart pounded in her

ears, becoming a roar rather than a pulse, then she heard him say, "Are you hot for me?"

She couldn't speak. He pulled back but did not release his hold on her. She watched as he took his swollen shaft in his free hand and stroked himself as he moved the invading finger slowly in and out of her soft-walled passage at the same time. She moaned more loudly, knowing she would be unable to stand the agony much longer. He flicked her sex, then drew his fingers away.

Caroline contracted at the loss; her hips thrust. "Please," she whispered.

He gave a throaty sound of pleasure; he leaned forward and licked her swollen bud. Only once this time, and too quickly. Her hips thrust toward him, violently, uncontrollably, jerking in needy wanting of his mouth. There again, on the hard nub of her desire, sucking, licking her to orgasm.

She shuddered with ecstasy.

He grabbed her hips, stilling her movement. "I asked you a question and it's only polite that you answer," he whispered against her wetness.

Still, she moaned and thrashed beneath him, against the cold steel wall of the elevator. "Please," she said.

"Not until you tell me," he answered her softly. "Neither of us can hold out much longer, so say it."

Helpless with need, her hips thrusting against his closed lips, she quivered above his now ungiving mouth. Her whole body was burning up. Her breasts felt heavy, and the moisture between her legs agitated her. Yet mingled with need was a sense of helplessness she had never felt before. It angered her and she grabbed herself, gasping, pressed the heel of her hand against the hard nub and the swollen slickness of her nether lips, trying to stop the wanton desire she felt for him. Him touching her. Him inside her, pounding hard and fast, with his thick, long length thrusting all the way into her stomach. She closed her eyes and shivered against her will. The aching between her legs seemed to slacken, then grew more intense.

She heard Landon inhale. Their mingled scent had become

a musky, commanding passion. He couldn't keep still. A drop of translucent moisture seeped out of the neat slit in his hard velvet tip. His pleasure muscle throbbed visibly as he watched—as she watched him. He stroked the length of himself, coaxing more of the fluid to come forth, and took the drops of moisture from the tip of his shaft carefully with the pad of his index finger. His right hand moved beneath her, up her stomach slowly, to touch the ebullition of life to each hardened summit in turn. She moaned, giving cries of need.

Caroline opened her eyes. He was staring at her, holding himself. His breathing was quickening. Her eyes flew wide. "No, please," she said breathlessly.

He stopped. But only long enough to shove his fingers inside her, though her pleasure was obviously not foremost in his mind any longer. He removed his fingers just as quickly and used her wetness to increase his own pleasure. She cried out in protest. Now his hardness was slick with her wetness, he was able to pull even harder on his thick shaft, faster, bringing himself closer and closer to release. She could not believe he was doing this to her. No!

Caroline clinched her teeth to stifle her cries. The throbbing between her legs told her he must give her an orgasm. He had to. She needed him, could feel her heat dancing beneath her skin.

"Stop teasing me, Landon. Please . You have to give me release. I—I am too hot. Don't do this to me. I want you inside of me."

"All you had to do was ask," he breathed against her heated skin.

Then he crushed her naked bottom in his fingers and he was kissing her all over. He kissed her under the arms and on the nipples and on the soft white skin of her belly. On the inside of her thighs, he skimmed rough fingertips over the back of her knees. He licked her breasts, sucked her rose-colored nipples until they ached.

She clawed at his head, pressing him against her and then pushing him back. A shock passed through her, collecting in a knot in her belly. Her mouth quivered, but she did not make a sound. *No*, she screamed inwardly. If she had not been so far gone, she would have killed him. Oh, but she was in heat.

She swallowed and licked her dry lips. "Then give it to me," she demanded.

He took hold of her thighs and wrapped both of her legs around his waist, slipped the tip of his root inside her, and stood. Commanding hands gripped her buttocks to hold her where he wanted, resting her back against the wall of the old elevator.

She shivered from the cold steel that pressed against her back. "Oh please, no more waiting." Her pulse was rioting in her throat, between her breasts, between her throat, and between the folds of her femininity. "Landon," she said, her hands trembling, her voice faltering. "All the way in—"

She did not have to ask.

His shaft was already moving more deeply inside her with conquest and speed where his fingers and tongue had probed. She was warm and moist from a prolonged state of sexual arousal, so when he pulled her hips to him, his long length plunged into her in one fluid, gratifying thrust.

Her bare legs wrapped tight around his strong hips and her arms snaked about his neck. She arched her back and clenched around his sex, as a long moan of pleasure escaped from her parted lips.

For a second Landon didn't breathe. She shivered as he kissed her mouth hard and withdrew his slick hardness, before driving home again. She was tight around him; he moved slowly and smoothly.

Caroline held her breath and tossed her head restlessly from side to side. When she quivered around his shaft, his thick black eyelashes fluttered with pleasure and he could no longer control himself. He raised his head, neck cording with the exertion, and fastened his mouth hungrily upon hers. In her tight folds, his flesh pierced her, stretched her, ground against her. His strokes were measured and hard.

His breathing was ragged. "Are you ready?"

Caroline twisted and turned in pleasure-pain as her climax approached. "Yes."

His hands were beneath her. He held her firmly against the wall, his shaft pumping and pounding against her, taking them both upward along the long-awaited spiral, until he heard her moaning, then her breath stopped and the little mouth of her shuddered around him in a chain reaction of tiny explosions.

Landon went rigid, couldn't hold back. Blazing, their shared pleasure erupted in waves, one after another, and he came, as she did, until they reached what seemed like the gates of eternity.

When they opened their eyes, she sank against the elevator wall, loving the crush of him against her.

He buried his face in the hair at her temple, his hands going to either side of her head to press her cheek against his. He said thickly, "Our sex life definitely has potential."

She shook her head emphatically.

"You'll change your mind," Landon declared, soft-spoken. The dark gaze that met hers across the elevator showing confidence. "You'll want me again; you know you will."

"No." Her voice was almost inaudible.

"I'll be ready when you are," he said, and it was clearly a promise.

She leaned back against the wall and closed her eyes. The rational part of Caroline thought this had to be dumbest thing she'd ever done. It had been compulsive, stupid—unnerving.

She wished he didn't kiss the way she had always remembered a man should kiss her, rough and very luscious, but affectionate in a way that swept her away. Then suddenly, out of nowhere, a wave of desire screamed again like a scorching wind. She wanted him badly.

What the devil was happening to her?

Obsession—

Furthermore, there wasn't even an elevator in the Magic 97 building.

—⋇⋄⋇—

Buzz! Buzz! Buzz!

Caroline was rudely yanked out of her fantasy dream by the alarm's incessant buzzing.

Eyes blinked and focused in on the woman standing in the doorway of her bedroom. Sandy Prator's face was drawn into an expression as affectionate and tolerant as it was concerned.

The housekeeper shook her head and clicked her tongue. "I was afraid this would happen again."

"What?"

"Exactly how dumb do you think I am?" She shook an index finger at her friend. "You've had another nightmare. I had hoped they had stopped, but as I can see they haven't. How long have you been keeping this from me?"

"Don't be absurd, Sandy. I haven't been keeping anything from you. It was, uh, simply a bad dream, and now it's over. It won't be happening again."

Caroline got out of bed, pulled on her robe and went into the bathroom to splash cold water on her face.

"You're upset. If the nightmare was that bad, why don't you share it with me? Talking it over might help." Sandy walked to the threshold of the bathroom and waited.

And it might not.

"Truly, I'm fine. I am also going to be late for work if I don't get dressed. Is the coffee ready?"

Sandy eyed her speculatively. "Yes."

"Great," Caroline said. "I'll be down in a minute."

As soon as Sandy left the room, Caroline put her head in her hands.

She knew divorcées were supposed to be notoriously horny. She just had no idea that it would ever happen to her. And it would never have, if she hadn't listened to that damned show. This was all Landon's fault!

Suddenly something the waiter at Marino's Fine Italian Restaurant had said earlier tonight came to her: "Vengeance and calamari were better served cold."

She would definitely have to remember that.

Chapter Five

That morning, the first edition of the Miller Beach Journal, a local tabloid, carried a front-page article that started with: "Magic 97's Landon Shafer launches lusty love-after-midnight show. Will it fly or die?"

When Sandy handed her the paper, which came to the house a little after seven-thirty, Caroline read and reread the headline, feeling as though she might very well have to go on tranquilizers before the day was out.

The doorbell rang before she even had time for a second cup of coffee. "Sandy, who is it?"

Forestalling a reply, Landon appeared in the kitchen doorway with a bouquet of yellow roses in hand. He held them out to Caroline and she stood, but did not take them. She brushed past him to refill her coffee cup.

Landon set the flowers on the table. "Caroline, I came to—to—"

She slammed her cup down on the counter, sending coffee on her, the counter, the floor, everywhere. "Don't try to butter me up. I am not in the mood. Besides, you need to save the treats for the horse you're going to ride."

"Fine!" he said, snatching the roses off the table and leaving.

Fine. She hated that blasted word. People said fine when they couldn't think of anything else to say. She, on the other hand, had no trouble thinking of another word.

Asshole! Now there's a word.

For the next few days and nights the atmosphere between Caroline and Landon, when they were together at the station, oddly went so much like the early years that she felt caught again in the old trap of uncertainty about what he was thinking.

Within a week, the ratings on overnights sharply increased. Everyone seemed to love his sexual fantasy format. Well, almost everyone. Caroline remained livid.

She kept quiet, though, now hoping the listeners would take care of the problem for her, but unfortunately, that had not happened. Apart from the verbal protests of very few religious organizations, there had been no major complaints. Certainly, no sponsors had threatened to pull their advertising, as she had assumed they would.

Not only did she feel Landon was just doing this type of show to get back at her, but he was ruining the station's image, an image it had taken her father years to build. Regardless of the show's apparent success, Caroline became determined to get Landon off the air.

But how? If she tried to talk to him, she knew it would be futile. Maybe her father's attorney could do something. Maybe Landon would let her buy him out.

That was the ticket! She dialed the telephone and put Keaton Osbrook on it.

Caroline turned off the engine and glanced at the gold watch on her wrist. Five o'clock. Almost time for the sun to set. The horizon crossed the eastern sky in radiant streamers of gold and scarlet. There was no rain. But she had hope for the future.

She looked at Sandy in the passenger's seat and forced a tiny smile. "If I'm lucky Landon will be off the air by Valentine's Day," she said in what she hoped was a cheery voice. "I've put out some feelers to see if I might be able to get him a job on the air at a station in Savannah. He likes it here, so he'll like it there. Savannah is beautiful, and it's less than a hundred miles away."

Sandy cleared her throat. "God willing, and the creek don't rise, he'll get a job in Savannah and like it."

"Everyone has an opinion—"

Caroline swung open the Jaguar's door and got out. The first of February on the coast of Georgia could, she knew from years of living there, be warm and mild. Today was cold, even in the late afternoon sun as she helped Sandy carry in the groceries from the car.

Sandy slid her a glance as they moved up the walk to the house. She was only half smiling. "That would be especially wonderful for you since Valentine's Day is also your birthday. One of the best presents you could receive, don't you think?"

"Why is it that I don't get the impression you think it is going to happen?"

"Let's just say that to me, it's kind of like a miracle. I'll have to see it to believe it."

In response, Caroline laughed softly.

Opening the back door, she placed the grocery bags on the counter and removed her jacket, laying it over the back of a chair. She strode to a window and stared out into the darkening sky. Just above a whisper, she said, "But if he doesn't agree to let me buy him out, I don't know what I'll do. We can't continue working together under the present conditions. And I can't let him keep doing this to the station."

"To the station or to you, Caroline?" Sandy asked.

Caroline turned around, but said nothing, which freed her friend to continue.

Sandy set her armloads of groceries on the kitchen table. "I'm not entirely comfortable with what I'm about to say, but if I'm to be straightforward, I'm afraid I have to tell you what I really think."

"And?"

"Your father's untimely death was a devastating blow to

you, coming after your miscarriage and then the divorce."

"True."

"Caroline, you told me yourself, you've had a severely broken heart. I know the show format that Landon picks to use is not one you are happy with, obviously, but it does seem to be going over pretty well."

"You listened to that program?" she all but shouted when she saw Sandy glance away.

"Well...yes. I did. But only a couple of times."

A couple of times, my butt.

"And I suppose you like the show's format?

Sandy turned her small hands, palms up. "I didn't not like it. And I can tell you, I haven't heard much gossiping about it either. At least, not yet." She paused and sighed. "My point is this. It's just possible you were hurt by your father leaving half of his money to Landon, and you're being unfair to him and his show because of it."

For a long time neither said a word. Finally, Caroline moved to the table and sat down. She focused on her clasped hands. "I would hope I am not that shallow."

"You still want me as an employee and friend?" Sandy asked.

Caroline looked up slowly to face her. "For heaven's sake, yes!"

"Then I have to ask you one more question, possibly an embarrassing question. Are you afraid Landon's show might actually be a success and prove you wrong?"

"Quite simply, I don't know. Maybe. I do know I hate the idea of that show being on the air. Hate it with a passion. I also have a very hard time believing he wants to do that type of format for any other reason than to assert his control. A control that my father assured when he set up the will the way he did. I loathe the idea of Landon controlling me in any way."

Sandy reached in the grocery bags and began to put canned goods away. "Landon is not Wayne," she reminded her.

"What is that supposed to mean?" Caroline got up to help.

Sandy put two cans of English peas on the top shelf of the

cabinet and turned to face her. "Only that not every man wants to control his woman."

"I am not Landon's woman," she said, tossing a five-pound sack of potatoes on the floor of the pantry, then slamming the door shut.

Sandy sighed as she folded the empty grocery bags and put them in the drawer. "I never said you were. The statement was nothing more than a figure of speech, Caroline. You know exactly what I meant."

Okay, maybe she did.

"I'm sorry," she said, leaning against the kitchen counter. "I do know what you meant. It's just that this whole thing is driving me crazy."

"Why? You moved Landon to overnights because his ratings were low on the morning show, which was a business decision. Am I right?"

Caroline folded her arms across her chest. "Your point?"

"I know you're concerned about the station's overall image, but nothing is going to happen. What could happen besides a few morally irate listeners who may or may not picket? Trust me, nothing will happen that hasn't happened already." Sandy paused to wave a hand.

"Regardless," she went on, "from what you tell me John and Melissa are doing great as Magic 97's Morning Crew. Landon's show is doing well, too. No one pulled advertising, as you feared, and his ratings are up. Why should that be driving you crazy? I should think you'd be ecstatic."

"Oh, Sandy, I don't know. Don't ask me, okay? The last week has been enough to drive me to an ice cream binge."

Sandy reached for her purse. "Fine."

Caroline cringed. There it was again. "Fine." The word was so, so—nothing. If she'd had an ounce of energy left, she might have made an issue of it, but she didn't, so she let it go.

"Thanks so much for supper tonight, Caroline. It was a nice change not to have to cook for you, or for me." Sandy smiled and winked.

"You're very welcome. I enjoyed it, too. I do love Italian

and Marino's always has the best lasagna. And calamari."

Sandy buttoned her coat. "You bet it does. Heck of a note for a restaurant in a town that prides itself on 'The Catch of the Day,' don't you think?"

Caroline chuckled. "As my father used to say, man cannot live on seafood alone."

"You can say that again! Listen, I have to run. See you tomorrow."

Just as Caroline headed toward the freezer and the ice cream carton, the back door reopened and Sandy popped her head in.

"The double-fudge ripple is on the top shelf, left-hand side of the freezer."

Caroline spun around. "Will you get out of here!"

"Just trying to help," Sandy mumbled as she closed the door again.

Caroline decided there was no doubt about it—she knew her too well.

—⊱❖⊰—

"I'll be double-dog damned," Landon said aloud to no one. He figured it was all right to talk to himself as long as he didn't answer.

Of all the things he had expected from Caroline Hunt, it had not been an offer to buy him out. Did she actually think he thought so little of her father? Sheldon Hunt, despite their lack of blood ties, had treated him well; his part of the station had been a gift of love. Landon could not, and would not sell it, even to Caroline.

He would call and tell her himself if he weren't so blasted mad, but he supposed she would know soon enough. After all, he'd told Keaton Osbrook plainly he would not sell, would never sell. Yes, he was sure she would know his answer before the hour was up.

"I didn't ask you if Landon was busy. I asked you if Landon was in his office!"

Okay, he was wrong. Caroline obviously had found out before the hour was up.

He left his office and found her standing in the reception area of the station, giving Marita what could only be described as "the evil eye." He saw Caroline, before she saw him. Saw her, and when she looked at him, he was shocked. Her face lighted and for a moment, she looked more as she had at sixteen.

"I've come to talk to you," she said. "I hope you're not too busy."

He made an instant decision, which was surprising, considering the confused leaping of his heart and the unwanted feeling of joy that flooded through him.

"Come into my office," he invited. "Unless you'd rather chew me out in yours?"

Caroline didn't like that remark if her narrow-eyed expression was any indication. "We'll be in Landon's office. Hold any calls. I don't want us disturbed," she said to Marita, who looked as if she was on the verge of a conniption fit.

He could just imagine Marita's face splitting and then flames shooting from her eye sockets. The receptionist, in the past, had been somewhat protective of him. Now was no exception.

He was forced to clear his throat and rub the sides of his mouth to keep from smiling. He and Caroline walked down the hall, where he opened the door for her. "After you."

She turned to face him, once they had privacy. "Why did you refuse to sell me your share in Magic 97?" she asked without hesitation, and marched in front of him. "I had Keaton offer you far more than it's worth."

Landon went behind his desk and sat down. "That may be true," he said. "But money is not the issue here."

"Is that so?"

He straightened a stack of papers and then looked at her. "You offered to buy me out because it's the only way you can think of to get me off the air."

She did not say, "You're right."

55

"Whatever the reason for my offer is none of your business," she told him. "I'd just like for us to come to a mutually beneficial agreement and get this over with."

When he stood, she was too close for comfort. Landon knew her too well. He knew the very shape of her body under her clothing. He knew the laughter that could brim in her sky-blue eyes, teasing him, though she was not teasing now. He knew the slow way a smile could begin at the corners of her mouth and then spread across her full lips. And he knew the way her laughter could burst out suddenly, engulfing him. This angry woman he knew less well. She had been like this when they were young. Before he had called a halt to puppy love and had gone away to college.

"Caroline," he said, his tone meant to caress, even though he didn't trust himself to touch her. "Can't we stop all this?"

She stood quite still. "All what?"

"We have both tried to forget about each other, but we can't."

She raised her hand as if to slap him, but he deflected the blow and pulled her to him.

"Let go of me," she said, pushing against his chest.

When he didn't, her angry expression turned to one of disbelief. "I hate you," she hissed through clenched teeth.

Landon's gaze moved over her lovely face. "No, you don't." He wanted to make love to her right there where they stood. "You might as well admit that you're not done with me yet. Not by a long shot. We will pick up again, only it won't be where we left off because we've both learned a lot since then, about life."

"Let me go, Landon!" she repeated. "I don't want—"

"Shut up, Caroline. Don't you think I know why you ended things between us? You were ashamed. Ashamed of what people would think of you and your father. Do you think I don't know how shocked the residents of Miller Beach would have been if they'd known the prim-and-proper Ms. Caroline Hunt had fallen in love with her stepbrother? Much less made love with him in her father's boathouse?"

She tried to escape, but he jerked her erect before him. "You know something, Caroline? I don't give a good damn what anyone thinks or says anymore. All I care about is us, and how we feel about each other. No matter how you try to hide it, there is something still between us."

"You're wrong. You—"

"No, I'm not. I can see it in your eyes when you think I'm not looking. I can see you wondering if it would be as good as it used to be. If we could make it this time if we told the world that we were picking up where we never should have left off all those years ago."

He took a handful of her long blond hair to tip her head back, to crush his mouth against hers while the tip of his tongue writhed on her tightly sealed lips, trying to force them open. She wedged a space between them, gripping his shirt while her fingers bored into his chest—yet she turned compliant in his arms.

His hands and lips were relentless, until he finally eased the pressure. The silken circles he drew on her lips at last unlocked them, and her body rose to accommodate his, while the hand clasping his shirt rested easy and began to caress. His tongue explored the interior of her mouth while one palm slipped beneath her elbow to boldly caress her breast.

But the contact had scarcely begun when Caroline, catching him off guard, abruptly pushed him away, spun around, and went to the window, where she stood trembling, angry, and he hoped, aroused.

Landon swore under his breath, yanked the door open, and stalked from the room, running into Marita, who stood outside the door.

"Holy—! What the devil are you doing out here?"

She smiled a bit tremulously. "Well, I was just bringing you today's uploads from Radio Star."

He pressed the knuckles of one hand against the palm of the other. "Listen, I don't have time right now to look at them. I'll get them from you later."

"Sure, Landon," she said and went back down the hall

toward the reception area.

Not five minutes after Landon's kiss, Caroline headed toward her car, her heart raising a furor in her body. Pulling out of the parking lot she gunned the Jag all the way into town. She cried for the dream-filled girl she'd once been and for the disillusioned woman she was now. She cried because in one split second, she had looked up into Landon's deep brown eyes and the tumult had sprung within her, an uproar of desire she'd never experienced during her marriage. She cried because she had to admit to herself that she was still in love with Landon.

And she cried for Wayne's child, which she'd lost.

And for Landon's child, which she would never have.

Chapter Six

If she had not been beside herself, Caroline would have noticed the tiny car in her rearview mirror sooner.

Did she know anybody who owned a beige VW Bug, about a '68 model? She didn't think so.

She looked in the rearview again and gave a long squinty-eyed look at the Volkswagen, but she could not make out the driver. Was she getting paranoid?

In point of fact she probably was, just a bit. Certain phone calls in the middle of the night with no one on the other end of the line had eroded her normal self-confidence. She had seen what looked like the same VW Bug a week or so before, behind her for more than a few blocks. And there were those odd news clippings that she had been getting by fax about women being victims of violent crimes. Or were they just news clips someone felt they ought to be commenting about on the air, but weren't? Until now, that had been exactly what she had believed. They were nothing more than news stories some amateur reporter was sending to the manager of the station.

So far, she had told no one about the VW Bug, or about the faxed clippings, which had stopped a couple of days ago. Perhaps, after all, they were just coincidences, the news clippings and the VW Bug appearing in her rearview mirror, twice.

She was just being silly. There were tons of old VW Bugs in every beach town, and this one was no different. Besides, this was a very small town. To catch sight of the same car, even twice in a two-week period, was not all that unusual.

Caroline sighed and drove grimly toward home. She was

losing her mind. That was all there was to it!

"Oh, man, have we got a live one here," Mike said indicating the telephone lines while they took a commercial break.

"I'm up for it if you are."

"I think it's that woman, Kitty, from the other night."

Landon shook his head. "We called her Kitten."

"Whatever. Just get ready, 'cause I'm throwing it to you in less than twenty seconds."

Landon shot him a thumbs-up and took a last swig of coffee as he watched the clock on the wall until the On-Air light illuminated and Mike tapped on the glass. He signed with his fingers—three, two, one—then pointed to Landon and, as always, mouthed, "You're on."

"Good morning, Miller Beach and the surrounding coastal areas! You're on the air with Landon Shafer and 'Sinful Secrets.' This is your favorite at work, or in this case, at play, station. Magic 97. Here's your chance to share your fantasies every weeknight from midnight until two. The number to call, 555-FANTASY, and we already have a caller. Hi, you're on the air."

"Who loves you, baby?" asked the deeply seductive voice on the other end of the line.

Landon lifted an eyebrow at Mike in the booth and laughed. "At this moment, I think I can safely say nobody."

"Don't count on that."

"You sound familiar, caller. Are you...Kitten?"

"I'm flattered you remember," she purred.

"How could I forget?"

Her laugh was throaty. "Are you ready to hear my sinful secret?"

"More than ready, Kitten."

"I'm lusting over a man who doesn't even know I'm alive. He may even be in love with another woman, though I'm not sure. What do you think I should do?"

"I think all's fair in love and war, Kitten. Give it your best shot. The way I look at it is, if you can take him away from this woman, he wasn't hers to begin with."

"I like the way you think, Landon."

"Do you have a fantasy about this man that you would like to share with us?"

"Yes, although I'm afraid it may be a little too wild for radio."

"There's not much we can't say on air after midnight, Kitten. Why don't you give it a try?"

"All right. If you're sure."

"Positive."

"Well...I go to his house late at night and he tells me to leave, while I've got the chance. Because I won't get another. 'What are you saying?' I ask."

Kitten purred. "He replies, 'I'm saying you're a very provocative woman and if you don't leave right now, I am going to lay you down on this bed and fill you with my flesh.' The words alone send my blood rushing through me as my heart knocks against my chest. I wish he hadn't put it that way. It sounded much too ominous.

"'Why am I so appealing to you?' I manage, after gathering a minimum of reason."

Landon took a sip of coffee.

Kitten continued. "He doesn't answer right away. When he reaches for me, a moan escapes. He lays down next to me and settles the inside of his thighs on the outside of mine. He presses his hardness against me and the feel of him scatters the last iota of wits I had just recently gathered. He grabs my hands then and glides them around his waist as he slants his lips over mine and brushes them with a featherlike touch. I instinctively respond by slowly running my hands up and down his warm muscular back.

"He kisses the curve of my throat before answering the question I had already forgotten I asked. 'You have possessed me since the first time I laid eyes on you,' he says. 'I am no longer going to try to control it.' I respond that I thought—"

"Go on," Landon encouraged.

"'You thought wrong,' he tells me. At his words, tiny sparks burst within me. Something strange happens, as strange as this wild part of the country we live in. I know it's up to me to stop it, if indeed it should stop. I shove desperately against his chest, needing the room to breathe. He allows me to put space between us, but slides a hand up the back of my neck as his fingers close around my hair.

"I watch his eyes race down my body. The intensity of his gaze causes me to gasp.

"'M—maybe,' I say, but he stops me with a shake of his head. He groans and pulls me close again. His hand actually trembles as he touches my cheek. He tells me, 'The lesson I have learned all those years ago was simple: caring for someone brought pain. But, there is something about you that has finally melted the ice that for so long had covered my heart.'

"'You had your chance to leave,' he says, and he means every word. The thick quality of his voice is wildly seductive. I swallow hard. I knew this was going to happen, and I release a sigh of relief. But instead of becoming calm, I feel a languid heat begin to coil inside my body."

Mike, from the other side of the glass, waved his hand as if to fan his face.

Kitten said, "'Before I ever touched you,' he says, 'I wondered if it was possible for your skin to feel as soft as it looks. And it is.' He kisses me as if he were starving for the taste of my mouth. I can see every little detail of the emotions that flickered in his eyes. First wanting, followed by resolve, then brief doubt, and finally just wanting.

"He leans forward, lets his face rest against my breast as he kisses it. He quivers and his eyelids drop shut.

"'Forgive me,' he mutters against my mouth, then he is pushing his tongue inside my mouth, twisting my face so that my head rests in his hand as he takes my mouth in his as if he has been hungering for an eternity.

"This is no gentle lovemaking, it is hard and needy, and I can do nothing but open my mouth to his and yield. His mouth is hot, wet, all-consuming. His hand seeks my breast through the layer of cloth and his touch burns a fiery path to my heart, causing my nipples to tighten deliciously. I cry out and he moans against my mouth. And the moan is one of pleasure, not regret.

"At the sound I stiffen and shake all over. He twists above me, yanking up my shirt and fumbles with his pants.

"'You are so very beautiful,' he whispers.

"Keeping as firm a hand on his lust as he can manage, he finishes stripping me, kissing each part of my body as he exposes it. He touches the tender inside skin of my thighs, and my heart skipped a beat. He is above me, gritting his teeth as he fights with the burning needs of his body to keep from doing more than he wants right now.

"Naked in the moonlight, he tells me I'm the most beautiful thing he has ever seen in his entire life. That my breasts are not overly big, but full and firm and white with lovely small nipples the color of strawberries in the summertime. He loves the way they jut forward from my small rib cage. He is breathing as if he had run a hundred miles. He bends down to draw a nipple into his mouth and suckle.

"I arch my back and moan, entwine my fingers in the back of his dark hair, and pull him more fully against me. My fingers tighten on his scalp the more he suckles. Not stopping to fall on top of me, he thrusts his throbbing shaft deep inside my body to pump out his lust between my legs as if it's the hardest thing he has ever done.

"My body is consumed in a sweet hot need, the likes of which I had never felt before. Wordlessly, I shift my gaze to him as he straightens. His eyes are very wide and they look more golden than brown. He tightens his hands around my waist and pulls back. He says he cannot lose all control yet. I can see his eyes on me, feel them, and hear the rasping of his breath. My gaze locks with his, and air rushes out of my lips in a long sigh as they part with excitement. I close my eyes and wait. He bends and touches the tip of his tongue to each of my eyelids. The unexpected caress steals my breath away.

"The evidence of his arousal produces a seething, twisting hungry fire in my core. He is heavy, full, hard, his member stirring with every beat of his heart. The telltale hardness of his body inside mine is unnerving and enthralling all at once. He tells me he needs me the way fire needs oxygen to burn.

"'I want you,' he says. The thickening of his blood with passion makes his voice low, almost rough. 'Lay your head back and let me learn the feel of all of you, your texture, the taste of your essence.' I do as he says and he withdraws from me. He slides down my body, then runs his hand up the inside of my thighs until he parts them.

"The touch of his mouth against my femininity is startling. My breath catches when he takes me gently between his teeth and flicks his tongue across my pulsating desire. At first I am too surprised to move, but as heat leaps within me, my thighs part further for him with a wanting such as I had never known was hidden within me. The repeated sensuous penetrating and retreat of his tongue deep within my moist folds sends cascades of shimmering sensations through my body. I think if there is any movement, I will die from the pleasure of it all. Almost as quickly as the unexpected caresses began, he retreats and raises back up to my face, placing his thighs between mine, and pressing the hard length of himself to my slick opening once more.

"'Did I displease you?' he asks.

"Nothing could have pleased me more, and I say so as the tip of my tongue traces the place where his teeth and tongue have touched mine.

"He says, 'Next time I will have you taste me.'

"'And, after I do?' I tease seductively. 'Then will you taste me again?'

"He laughs, and says, 'Until you can no longer stand it.' The heated promise in his eyes causes a liquid fire to leap even deeper within me and escapes my softness.

"A low sound rips from my throat as he moves his hand between my folds and I feel the living heat within his palm. He watches with measured eyes as the fire created by his touch consumes me. Lowering his face, he seduces my mouth with slow, sure strokes that echo those of his hand. He makes love to me with words. Then slides his wide, strong hands down the backs of my thighs and with one swift motion he lifts me to his waist. I clutch his shoulders as he positions me and I instinctively wrap my legs around him in a flurry of need.

"Then he claims me anew. Drives deeply within. He throws his head back and gives a fevered moan. His taking of me is slow and tormenting and brings me even greater pleasure. I am instantly intoxicated. As he moves inside me, withdrawing and gently filling me again, I make sounds like a woman in delirium and he gasps for air like a man near drowning. My body heats by degrees and I move around him, twisting, urging him on, I toss my head from side to side as my hands frantically clutch his back.

"The pleasure, when it peaks this time, is so extreme that it sends my soul racing far above the heavens on crazy streaks of bright light, so intense that I think I can't stand it, but finally I buckle and my soul returns to my body and I fall back to earth sated and exhausted.

"I return just in time to see him throw his head back and stiffen in my arms. After several deep, desperate thrusts, he gives a loud cry and convulses inside me before exhaustion claims him and his knees give way. Then we lay there together for a long time, breathless and trembling—"

Kitten paused for a long moment, before she asked, "Well, what did you think?"

For the first time since Landon had first developed this show's format in his mind, he thought Caroline might actually have been right. About everything.

He took a deep breath. "Kitten, that was something else."

"Do you really think so?" she asked on a mere breath of a whisper.

"I think I can speak for all the after-midnight listeners when I say, thanks for sharing." Landon paused to push the lighted button to end Kitten's call. "Now we're going to play a little sensual music for you right here on Magic 97, so stay tuned."

As soon as Mike gave him the all-clear sign, Landon snatched off his earphones, stood up and raked a hand through his hair.

Mike jumped up and stuck his head through the door. "Holy-moley!"

"You can say that again."

⟶≈⋄≈⟵

Just after Landon went off the air at two A.M., Marita opened the door and poked her head inside the studio.

He blinked. "What are you doing here this time of night?"

"I brought you more uploads from Radio Star."

Landon waved good-bye to Mike, who was walking past Marita out the door. "At this hour?"

"I couldn't sleep. I thought maybe I could talk you into going out for some breakfast."

"Sure, why not? We can take my Cherokee."

"That sounds like a deal."

They left.

The Waffle Hop, just south of the beach on Vermilion Street was a nice quiet place to sit and talk, especially at two-thirty in the morning. Marita and Landon sat drinking coffee at a booth for two not far from the long counter across from the man flipping eggs on an open grill. Landon enjoyed the informal, friendly, almost funky atmosphere of the place.

Many early mornings, after going off the air, Landon and Mike would stop here on their way home to have something to eat and drink, and to talk about the show. Listeners knew that and would join them frequently.

Landon liked to think of his visits to the Waffle Hop as a sort of roundtable discussion with his audience. In that way, he got the listeners' likes, dislikes, and a lot of input as to what they thought in general about the show. But this time it was different. The place was pretty much empty tonight. He had Marita for company.

Marita sat across the booth, nursing her coffee, devoid of expression. He had to admit she was an elegant sight. With her hair tied back tightly in a ponytail with a gold ribbon around it and her face devoid of heavy makeup, she resembled a movie star—a kind of sixties-era Liz Taylor. Only she had brown eyes instead of violet.

"Are you hungry?"

"A little," she said in her husky voice.

"Should I order for both of us?"

"Yes, that would be fine."

Landon turned to give their order to the waitress. He ordered a refill and selected a waffle for both of them, then leaned forward to ask Marita, "What made you decide to come down to the studio?"

"I told you. I couldn't sleep." She closed her eyes, her mouth stiffened, and a tic tugged at her upper lip. She patted her mouth with a napkin and slipped it in her lap.

Landon glanced at her suspiciously and shrugged.

"I overheard your…your argument with Caroline today, not that I was listening or anything. I wouldn't want you to think I'm an eavesdropper. It's just that—it's just that—well, I think everyone heard it."

Landon reached across the table and patted her hand. "Don't worry about it. Stuff happens. Besides, that was not the first argument we've ever had."

Marita lowered her eyes and nodded. "I know. And I think she's being unfair to you."

"Really?"

"Oh, yes. You are such a great talent. She should appreciate you instead of constantly criticizing."

"I don't know if it is so much a criticism on her part as much as it is a conflict of interest."

"I think you are being generous," Marita said quietly.

He gazed at her. She'd been with the station for several months. She had once confessed a mild crush on him to his producer, Mike, when she first started.

Landon sat back and chuckled. "I'm happy to hear you're

in my corner, Marita, but I'd keep it to myself if I were you. Caroline is the station manager, after all."

"Oh, I would never express my personal opinions at the office," she said, flushing.

The waitress delivered their waffles. They watched in silence as she refilled their coffee cups. When the waitress moved out of earshot, Landon continued. "You're very sweet, Marita, do you know that?"

There was a long silence. She sampled her food. Then she looked up again.

"I'm glad you think so," she said quietly.

He was having a surprisingly good time. Something he'd needed. Although he wasn't up for a romance, it wouldn't hurt to ask her out for a dinner between coworkers.

"Would you be interested in dinner tomorrow night?" he asked.

Suddenly Marita looked up. Landon was puzzled by the expression on her face. It was as if she were a whole different person for a moment. He tried to figure out what it was, but he could not.

"What is it? Is something wrong?"

"No, nothing," she said, and the expression disappeared as quickly as it had come.

"Can I call you tomorrow then—about dinner?"

Marita smiled brightly. Too brightly, somehow. "Yes, please. I look forward to it."

Chapter Seven

"Ow!"

"What the—" Caroline shot down the hall and into the bathroom. Barely inside, she skidded to a halt and stared at Sandy, who stood in front of the mirror and extended a long strand of hair straight up toward the ceiling.

"What are you doing?"

Sandy snorted. "Getting rid of a few gray hairs. Do you *mind?*"

Caroline made a *tsk-tsk* sound, then pointed an index finger. "Do you know that for every one you pull out, two more grow in its place?"

Sandy dropped the clump in her hand and turned toward Caroline, rubbing her scalp. "Well, that explains why I have so many."

"Geez. I was just kidding. That's only an old wives' tale."

Sandy put her fists on her hips. "The gray hairs on my head sure seem to be appearing more rapidly by the minute. And they are pretty well anchored, too, I can tell you. When I pull out one of those wiry suckers, it hurts all the way on the other side of my head. Someone's wife must be trying to tell me something."

Caroline laughed so hard she could hardly catch her breath. "Does that mean you are going to quit pulling out your gray hair?"

"Yeah...for the moment anyway," Sandy said with a wink.

—∗⟨⟩∗—

It was a beautiful morning, not too cold. On the way to work, Caroline noticed the blue sky and the few clouds that rode high. The latter looked to be scudding eastward happily and blissfully. She glanced out the open window of her Jaguar to the Atlantic on her left. Ahead, there was hardly anyone on the road.

She'd left for work earlier than usual and so she'd missed the morning traffic by a few minutes. After a couple more blocks, she drove by the park. Even the sound of Atlantic waves rolling in seemed a relaxation. This was a time when she could let her mind dwell on details that were not nice, on complexities that arose to be solved, on contradictions that could be explored and neutralized. Driving was the best place to spend quality time—when she needed it with herself.

Then she heard a different kind of roaring, different from the surf. Another car? Probably. But where was it? Getting ready to pull out in front of her? No. Behind her?

Looking in the rearview mirror, she saw nothing. She flipped on the radio and began marking the beat of a song with her fingers on the wheel. Then she increased her speed on an area of straight road, which would take her right to the station.

The odd roaring persisted. It could be the echo of her engine, distorted by the asphalt of the road. As always, she was alone.

One thing had become quite clear over the past few days. The stress Caroline had been under had finally become too much to deal with. She was rapidly arriving at a point where she had to seize hold of her wits, or be forced to seek professional help.

The problem? She wasn't the type of woman who would enjoy baring her soul to an entire stranger. She'd been handling her problems by herself for the past two years, working her way through them, bit by bit.

She stopped at a red light. Magic 97 was up about two blocks on her right. She turned the radio down and listened closely, hearing little but the roar of the Jaguar's engine and her own pumping heart.

The light changed; she started moving again. For a block and a half she drove, then pulled smoothly into the parking lot of the station.

She noticed a car behind her. Not the VW, thank goodness. Still the driver of the blue sedan pulled in the same parking lot. Who was it? No one else would be coming to work this early. When she'd left the house, she could have sworn she was ready for anything. But she wasn't ready to die in a drive-by shooting!

A car door slammed; her heart jumped into her throat. Sensing someone near her car, she rolled up the window and pressed the electric button that locked all the doors. She was too afraid to look.

"Are you all right?" a woman asked from the other side of the window. A familiar voice, but Caroline couldn't place it. And she could not bring herself to look.

"Y—yes," she said, closing her eyes and struggling for calm. Yet she knew that the voice had not been hostile; it was one of apparent concern.

"Do you need some help?" the voice continued.

Caroline pulled herself together and looked out her window at Marita Taubold, who had obviously arrived early for work, too.

Well, she thought. *Stress has finally snapped my noodle.*

Exiting the Jaguar, she looked around. "Where's your car, Marita?"

"In the shop. I had a friend drop me off. That's why I'm here so early. My friend starts work an hour before I do."

Caroline expelled a breath. "I see."

On the heels of having her wits scared out of her, unnecessarily, Caroline entered the station with less energy than she had felt in months. The only good thing about this morning?

She wouldn't have to see Landon. With his overnights spot, they now crossed paths very little, which was just peachy with her. Especially, after the recent confrontation in her office.

She sent The Morning Crew on a remote to Brunswick and the station was quiet after they left. The morning passed without anything more happening, although she kept a weathered eye out for any more of those blasted faxes.

She ate an apple at her desk for lunch. Even though she'd calmed down a bit, she still had no desire to risk getting in her car and driving across town on the off chance she might catch sight of a VW Bug in her rearview mirror.

Shortly after lunch Caroline stared morosely at the keyboard of her computer, trying to force the words into reasonable sentences, but her mind stayed stubbornly blank and so did the monitor. She had always enjoyed her job, had used it as therapy even. Why did she now have so much blasted trouble focusing on work?

Dumb question.

Just then a knock at her door took her attention. "Yes?"

Marita poked her head into Caroline's office.

"Come in. Come in." She motioned to the receptionist. "What can I do for you?"

"Things are quiet today and I was just wondering—"

"Wondering what?"

"If you would mind if I left a little early today?"

Caroline sat back in her chair and folded her hands in her lap. "Something special you'd like to do?"

Marita shifted her weight from one foot to the other. "I have a date tonight. Since I have to take a cab home—"

Caroline smiled and raised a hand like a stop sign. "Say no more. Leave whenever you feel you need to."

Just as the woman started to exit the office, Caroline asked, "Anyone I know?"

The receptionist swiveled around to face her. "I'm sorry?"

"Are you going out with anyone I know? What I mean is, is it someone from the station?"

"Yes, it is." A slight smile accompanied a slightly puffed-up chest.

Caroline lifted her coffee cup and brought it to her lips for a sip.

"Landon is taking me out for dinner. I'm really looking forward to it. I only hope he is as well."

Caroline coughed, then choked.

Marita rushed forward and patted her on the back. "Are you all right?"

Disappointment made her stomach go hollow, but Caroline was very careful not to look at her, or else her shock might be mirrored in her face.

"I'm fine." She pushed the helping hands away, realizing she'd uttered her most hated word. "The coffee just went down the wrong pipe. It happens to people all the time. Now go on and get out of here before the day is over."

If Landon wanted to date Marita Taubold, why should she care? She didn't! Or did she?

—⚜—

When Caroline arrived home that evening she broke down and told Sandy everything. Well, almost everything.

She got a simple laugh in reply.

"Sandy Prator, I cannot not believe it. I bare my soul and you laugh? Some friend!"

"Sorry, but I'm not laughing at you." The housekeeper sat heavily in a kitchen chair. "I'm laughing at that fact you think you're on the verge of some sort of breakdown."

Caroline moved to press both palms to the table's surface and leaned forward. "And you don't think extreme paranoia is any cause for alarm?"

"In your case, no, I do not." A brow arched. "I think you're overreacting like you always do. Not that it's you fault. You do come by it quite naturally."

Caroline threw her hands in the air. "Come by what naturally?"

"Overreacting, silly."

"Oh, hogwash!"

"I'm serious, Caroline. I've known you ever since your father first moved to Miller Beach, and I can honestly say you are an overreacter. You can certainly make too much of stuff. And your father was a nut." Sandy paused to raise a hand in the air. "A nice nut, mind you, but still a nut."

If Caroline hadn't recognized at least some merit to what Sandy had just said, she would have been offended. As it was, maybe her friend might be right after all. Yes, sanity was relative. Under the circumstances, she could safely believe she had reacted normally.

Still, at this moment, she was ready for a change of any kind. Better or worse, she would take whatever came first.

Sandy smiled then. "If I were you, I'd go on to bed now and sleep in late tomorrow morning. For once in your adult life, don't worry about what time you get to the station. You need the rest. I'll even bring you breakfast in bed if you want."

"Go in late?"

"Why not? I'll make biscuits and gravy."

"Well, I am the boss—"

"All right, Caroline. Sleep well." Sandy moved to kiss her swiftly on the cheek, patting her on the shoulder at the same time, something she had never done before, then left.

Caroline locked the front door and walked slowly up the stairs, one step at a time. She padded along the hallway to her bedroom. It was getting darker every moment; she had to turn on a light to see her way around. As she leisurely undressed she heard the muffled sound of the surf in the distance and a breeze that blew in from a partially open window. It was cold and not yet fully dark. She closed the window and pulled the curtains to darken the room, but the last bit of red-gold sunset found its way through the gaps at the sides.

The ensuing silence being far from golden, it depressed her. She stepped into the shower, wondering what Landon was doing now. Was he at home alone, or out with Marita? What a stupid question! Of course, he was still out with Marita. Their evening had probably just begun.

While she stood beneath the massaging heat of steaming water, she couldn't help but wonder—If he were to see her naked, after all these years, would he think she had a good body?

With a sigh she turned off the water, pulled a plush towel from the nearby rack, and began drying herself—she was suddenly exhausted and very lonely. When she crawled into the big queen-size bed, her legs were weary, and she had a niggling pain in the small of her spine. She flipped on her back with her eyes closed, thankful for the cool white comfort of clean sheets. Thankful for Sandy.

She wished her mind could relax like her body, where she could pass into sleep with no roar of the Atlantic coming into shore, whirling in a sea of faces. She pressed her hands over her eyes, but the visages of Landon, Marita, and even her deceased father would not go away.

Caroline Lee Hunt, get that blasted man out of your mind. And just what do you think the good people of Miller Beach would say if you were seen with your former stepbrother, especially when your divorce is scarcely one year old?

Be that as it may, it still hurt, thinking of another woman with Landon, as she had once been. She remembered his dark wind-whipped hair and his tanned fingers on her arm, the soft invitation in his voice. And his lips—those lips hadn't changed a bit in all these years. Then she thought of the empty house, with superimposed images of the two of them in the living room, the kitchen, and the bedroom—

But then, remembering how many other women had probably done the same thing—and more—with Landon Shafer, she shook his image from her mind and reached for the remote.

To end the silence, Caroline flipped on the TV. Still in the back of her mind, she thought about the beige VW, but that concern was pretty much shoved aside by thoughts of what Landon might be doing on his date with Marita.

Turning on her side, Caroline pulled the extra pillow into her arms and held it tight. She fell asleep sometime later watching an old Loretta Young movie.

Chapter Eight

Mmm! Caroline's body and heart and soul smiled. First magnolias and now spicy bay rum. She inched up her chin a notch. Her bedroom suddenly had such wonderful smells— like something from childhood—

And a very interesting accoutrement. Landon. His body hair was rough, but springy and soft. She lay curled to his hard and sinewy legs. She reveled in his muscular thighs, firm hips.

Ah...such a wonderfully lazy movement of a thumb upon her flesh as her nipple was tenderly fanned into a tight peak. Responding to his touch, her lips parted slightly. Such delightful hands cupping her breasts.

"Mmm," she breathed again.

Then his fingers traced around her areolas. Bending his head low, he stroked the very tip of her breasts with his warm, wet tongue and she felt a fiery rush of excitement. Her back arched as all ten fingers clutched his hair. "Don't stop."

"Only to make it better for you, my dear."

He tilted his head, adjusted the angle, then his tongue invaded her mouth with thrusts that took her breath away. She loved the way he tasted, the way he smelled, the way he touched her, the way he felt beneath her fingers. She hadn't thought it could get any better...even better than the first time...better even than the wonders he had shown her all those years ago. She wrapped her arms around his strong neck and reveled in the way his mouth seemed to draw out every breath in her body and then give it back again...with so much more each time.

His mouth gently ate its way up her neck. His tongue play-fully batted her earlobes as he slid her gown over her thigh, lin-gering to caress the softness that enclosed her passionate need. She kept his hand there and pulled her nightshirt the rest of the way over her head.

He smiled and crushed her to him, his hand trapped between them. She moved her body more fully against his. His touch was such perfection, she was compelled to draw him closer and wrap her legs around him, to feel the extent of his desire nestled against her greatest fire.

Suddenly, his head lowered to kiss her as he slipped the tip of himself just inside the wetness of her opening and thrust inside. She welcomed him. His fullness, and the way he fit her together with him, was altogether miraculous. He kissed her long and deep; she tightened her arms around him, surren-dering to the dewy caresses of his mouth. She crossed her legs over his hips, then sighed and arched upward, to bring him even closer and deeper, to hold him fast in the cradle of her pelvis.

How exquisite the pleasures of their joined bodies! How wonderful it was to have him here, with her, giving and taking the joys of their bodies—

Caroline thought she must surely be spiraling her way toward the heavens, until—

Suddenly, he pulled away to the accompaniment of rapid gunfire and what sounded like John Wayne shouting orders to the troops in the background—

John Wayne? What?

Caroline, the television blaring, yanked open her eyes and blinked to focus on the ceiling. She shook her head, astound-ed to find herself alone in bed again with nothing more than TV to keep her company. Not to mention the fact she was now more angry and frustrated than she had ever been in her life.

She closed her eyes, threw her forearm over her face, and

groaned. Obviously, her feelings for Landon were stronger than she'd ever acknowledged. Had she not kept dreaming about him, she probably would never have recognized her dilemma; she wouldn't have been forced to. But as it was, she had no choice but to face her feelings.

And when she did, she cried.

—❈—

Twenty-five miles from town, glad Landon had insisted on dinner at the Gaslight Inn, Marita figured this must be heaven. At least as close to heaven as she had ever been. It was far away from Miller Beach and just about everything else...including Caroline and that damned radio station.

On the way to a table, Landon picked up a beer at the bar. Marita ordered a rum and cola with a twist of lime, then followed Landon to the patio.

He reached for a chair and pulled it out for her. "Have a seat."

As a gentle breeze stirred her hair, she giggled like a sophomore. "You are so sweet."

Landon sat down and moved his chair closer to hers. Wordlessly, he shifted position. Now their legs were touching, just a bit. He glanced at her and she smiled. That was all it took, a touch, a smile, and everything changed for her.

She leaned forward until her firm breasts were resting comfortably on the table. She watched him look between them and she returned his smile. He cleared his throat, downed what was left of his beer, and ordered another.

For three hours they dined and danced, drank and danced, and Marita fell madly in heat. She had matched him drink for drink—or so she led him to believe. Landon was wonderful. The food was wonderful. Everything was wonderful.

She gazed at him across the table. "I meant to tell you how sorry I am you're having so much trouble with Caroline over the show and all."

"She has been a pain in the butt, that's for sure," Landon

allowed. "You know, I really don't see why she has to be so difficult all the time. I should think she would be happy. The new ratings book is just out. The show is two full points above my best expectations."

"And that's only the first ratings book of the year. Wait until the summer one comes out. The next thing we know, you'll be giving the big boys a run for their money."

Landon laughed. "Oh, I'm sure."

"You're the one bringing the most money into the station. I'm not deaf. I hear the salespeople talking. Everyone wants to advertise on your show."

His eyes brightened. "Maybe not everyone. Although I've added to the advertisers, pulling in bigger and better ones. And you're right about my show earning the most money."

"Caroline should be grateful. Why, if you wanted to, you could leave Magic 97 and go to a bigger market. Like Panama City."

Landon raised both eyebrows. "And compete with 'Amos in the Morning?' I don't think so!"

"Why do you think he's in Panama City? Howard Stern kicked his butt in New York City. You could too—"

"I am not Howard Stern, Marita."

"You are to me."

Landon cleared his throat. Then nature apparently called, and he excused himself. Marita took advantage of his back being turned to let her gaze wander down his body in a lingering trail, coming to a rest on his tight, muscular behind, which was tantalizingly outlined in close-fitting jeans.

He later returned to suggest it was time to leave.

She could tell by his expression—he sensed her reluctance to bring the evening to a close. But did he understand? After all, they had enjoyed a beautiful dinner together. Yet it had started to end. If she told him what she had in mind for later, how would he react?

They were both quiet on the drive back to her apartment; she used the time to rehearse her speech mentally. As they drove past the complex's entrance, she shifted in her seat to face him.

When he pulled into a parking space and turned off the Jeep's engine, she asked, "Have I done something wrong?"

"Why would you think that?"

"It's just that I had a really nice time this evening, but right before we left the restaurant you seemed to tense up and I assume it was my fault. Did I misunderstand? Weren't you enjoying my company as much as I was yours? I thought—"

He pressed a finger to her lips. "Hush. I had a great time with you tonight, okay? It's just that all good things must come to an end." He smiled. "Now let me walk you to the door."

His words gave her encouragement.

Once at the door, she faced him and tried to make her tone matter of fact. "Would you like to come in? I have a lot of videotapes. We could watch a movie. It isn't really very late."

He must have sensed what she was up to; he glanced at her with a questioning gaze. "I'm pretty tired, Marita."

Distress flared briefly within her before she put on her best pout. "Just for a moment? One nightcap maybe?"

It worked. His expression softened. "Sure. I guess I can do one drink."

Yes! She would fix his drink, a strong one. And just before he was finished, she would make her move.

Once firmly inside her apartment, she flicked on a lamp.

Landon sat on the couch as she went to mix the drinks. "I hope you like whiskey. It's all I have."

He thereafter took the three fingers of aged bourbon on the rocks that she handed him.

Eeow! Three fingers? Landon figured to sip the strong drink Marita handed him, given that he didn't make a habit of taking his booze neat. But he knew he'd already upset Marita. He had no desire to hurt her feelings again. He watched her select a tape and slip it into the VCR. With her own glass in hand, she took several steps toward him and sat near him on the couch. She picked up the remote and started the movie. *My word,* Landon thought. She'd chosen a porn flick!

She must have thought that since his radio show format was a sex fantasy call-in show that he would like to watch this sort of film. He forced himself not to clear his throat and downed a good half of his drink.

Apparently as the movie progressed, so did Marita's libido. She unbuttoned the top two buttons of her blouse and revealed an inordinate amount of cleavage. She also took an ice cube from her glass and began running it over the skin of her neck, down between her breasts...

She tilted her chin. He cocked a brow. He liked her small, pert mouth. And her tiny tipped-up nose.

"It's hot in here, don't you think?" She spoke the words softly.

Landon eyed her, and he couldn't help his stirrings of interest. Thinking better about it, he adjusted his position on the couch. "I don't think it's hot at all."

"I beg to differ." She glanced toward the window. "The night is warmer than I thought it would be. Maybe I should turn the air conditioner on." The ice went up her neck again and she shook her hair away from her shoulders. "I do feel a bit better now. If you're sure you're comfortable..." She put the remainder of the half-melted cube in her mouth and sucked.

Landon nodded but didn't say anything and finished his drink.

She leaned toward him. "Would you like another?"

When he shook his head, Marita gathered his empty glass and set it aside. She sat there with her gaze full of desire. Then she picked up the remote and lowered the volume on the TV before scooting closer to him on the couch.

"I really am glad you're here," she said, placing a gentle hand on his thigh.

Landon had to keep himself from jumping up and leaving right then. Marita might be an attractive woman, available and willing—boy, was she willing!—but if he had a lick of sense, he'd get the hell out of Dodge before things went too far.

He simply wasn't interested.

It was too late.

Her hands wove in his hair, pushing it back from his forehead as she kissed him, opening his lips, bidding him to enter. Straining against him, she pressed him backward against the couch. Her body rose and fell rhythmically, as if desperately seeking to fulfill an undeniable need that throbbed within her.

Landon quickly pulled out of her grasp, and stood. He then shifted his gaze to the woman he now towered over. The look she gave him in return wasn't a kind one.

"This has nothing to do with you, Marita." He stepped back. "And everything to do with me."

She trembled as if her anger was growing. "Really?" It was more of a statement than a question.

Landon straightened his shirt. Shoving his hands in his pockets, he said, "Yes, really."

"That's odd. I think it has something to do with someone else entirely," she said as she sat up and crossed her arms over her chest, without bothering to rebutton her blouse.

"What the devil are you talking about?"

"You mean *who*, don't you?"

Irritation crept up to his collar. "All right then, Marita. Have it your way. Who do you mean?"

"Caroline."

"That is crazy." Wasn't it?

"I don't think so. Everyone in Miller Beach knows you two used to have a thing for each other."

They did? Landon waved a deceptively dismissive hand. "I can assure you what happened between you and me tonight had nothing to do with Caroline."

"Are you sure?"

Hell no, he wasn't sure. "I don't want to mislead you. It wouldn't be fair."

"Mislead me?"

He returned to the couch and touched her cheek. "Listen,

82

Marita. I find you very attractive. What man wouldn't? But I'm not ready to make any type of commitment."

Her lips drew into a soft smile. "Did I ask you for a commitment? How do you know I'm not after you just for sex?"

Landon laughed gently. The look on her face spoke volumes. "I guess I don't."

He leaned forward, impelled by some force he was only vaguely aware of, and lifted her chin with his fingertips until he was gazing into her soft brown eyes. "I don't understand you at all, Marita Taubold. One minute you're like a teenage girl. The next you're as aggressive and blunt as any woman I've ever known."

He continued to gaze into her eyes, surprised that he hadn't turned and left. And surprised at himself for touching her.

"Can't we just be friends for now?" he asked. "See each other on some sort of neutral ground, so to speak?"

She pulled away but maintained eye contact a moment longer. "What are you afraid of? Me—or yourself?"

"Gotta go." He strode from the apartment, closing the door behind him. He glanced back. Why did he avoid a relationship with her?

He had a reason. He had a feeling she wasn't the type of woman he could ever have simply as a friend. Because he didn't need an entanglement in his life right now? Or because there was someone else he wanted to be entangled with?

He got into the Jeep and drove straight to the one true bar in Miller Beach.

Marita watched him leave from her window. She had to admit the night had not gone exactly as she'd hoped. But as is said, nothing is over until the fat lady sings. And she sure as hell did not hear any singing!

She changed from skirt and heels to jeans, sneakers, and hooded sweatshirt, then headed out the door for the beach.

Once near the water, the stiff salty breeze whipped her hair until she adjusted and tied the hood of her jacket, confining the errant strands. She took a deep breath of bracing air and strolled resolutely to her destination.

The past was nothing to her, Marita decided. It offered no lessons that she cared to learn. The future was a mystery that she had never attempted to penetrate. Only the present had any significance to her, and it was hers.

Chapter Nine

Landon awakened from a too-much-to-drink-induced deep sleep. It was difficult to focus on the details of reality around him. But dominating everything seemed to be the screeching of a bell.

The telephone, he thought drowsily, trying to pry his eyes open in the pitch-dark of his bedroom. Reaching to click on the bedside lamp, he knocked over the clock radio. He groaned and grabbed the receiver.

"What?"

"Landon! Landon!" cried the hysterical voice on the other end of the line. "I'm so glad you answered! I was so afraid the machine would pick up!"

"Who is this?" he asked, still trying to focus.

"Marita!"

He sat up and shoved a hand through his hair. "What's wrong? Why are you screaming?" He reached to the floor and retrieved the clock radio. Three o'clock in the morning.

"Oh, Landon—Landon, I've been robbed!"

Robbed?

He tossed the tangled covers aside and tried to clear his head. "What?" He swung his legs over the side of the bed.

Marita heaved a ragged sigh. "Someone broke into my apartment. It was awful. I was sleeping and something woke me. A noise—I heard a noise in the living room and I got out of bed. Then I saw a man—a dark figure rummaging through my things. Oh, Landon...He heard me. He saw me. And then he hit me. He hit me!" She paused to sniffle more than once.

"Now, the police are here."

"Calm down, Marita. I'll be right over. You said the police are there, correct?"

"Yes, they're here. But you don't need to come over. I—I'll be fine. I just needed to talk to you...there's nothing like the feeling that someone you don't know just went through your things—"

"I said I'll be right over. Just sit tight."

"All right."

Within minutes Landon had yanked on jeans and a T-shirt, and was jumping into his Cherokee. He twisted the ignition key, stamped on the brake, and shoved the gearshift into reverse. Hitting the accelerator, he headed for Marita's apartment.

The Jeep shot forward like a missile. It fishtailed into the middle of the street and careened around the next corner without benefit of brakes to slow its turn.

By the time Landon reached the entrance to apartment complex, he could see patrol cars, their lights flashing. The same spot he had parked earlier that same night was empty; he drove quickly into it and stopped. Out of the Jeep, he ran across the pavement to the sidewalk.

Two police officers stood just inside Marita's door.

One of the men in uniform said, "Landon," recognizing him.

He thought the officer's name might be Bob, but he wasn't sure, although he did remember they had attended high school together. "Hey, man. What's going on here?"

"On the record or off?" asked Officer "Bob" with a smile.

"Marita is a friend of mine. This has nothing to do with the station."

The officer looked at the pad of paper in his hand. "Oh, that's right. She works at Magic 97, too, doesn't she?"

Landon nodded and glanced inside the apartment. Two other uniformed men were milling around a broken window as if looking for evidence. "Is she okay?"

"Sure, just a bit shook up is all."

"Are you certain? She told me on the phone the man hit her."

The officer placed his hands on his well-rounded hips. "You know how women exaggerate. It was really more of a shove than a hit, I think. Didn't see any bruising. But there may be some come morning light."

"Landon! I'm so glad you're here!" Marita raced across the room and threw her arms around his neck, and squeezed.

Landon patted her back reassuringly. When she stepped back, he saw her slightly swollen lip. But the officer was right. No mark, at least not yet.

Marita pulled a wad of tissue from her pocket and blew her nose.

"Do you want me to take you to the hospital?" Landon asked.

"No." She shook her head. "The cops already offered. I'm all right. Really."

"I still think a quick run down to Phoebe General would be a good idea," he said, looking over at the officer he had just been talking to.

The officer cocked his brow in Marita's direction and shrugged. "It's always best to be checked out after something like this happens."

"Landon, I don't want to go."

And it was at that point she broke down. She leaned forward, laid her head on his shoulder, and began to weep. With her body racked by long, shuddering sobs, she could barely catch her breath.

When he put his arms around her, she finally stopped crying.

"Officer," Landon said. "How much longer should all this take? Has she already given you a statement? I'd like to take her home with me for the rest of the night."

"Sure, Shafer. No problem. I have her statement right here and I've notified the building's maintenance man about the broken window. He'll be up to fix it first thing in the morning. As soon as the investigators inside are finished, which shouldn't be long now, we can all be on our way. As I said before, I truly think this was nothing more than a random act. This intruder won't be back."

Landon turned to Marita. "If you want to take a sick day tomorrow, I am sure Caroline will understand."

"No, no," she said emphatically. "I want to go to work. If I don't I'll just sit around all day and drive myself insane thinking about all this. Believe me. I would much rather be at the station."

"All right. If that's what you really want, I'll wait here while you change out of your robe and nightgown, and gather the things you'll need in the morning."

Within minutes, the police had collected the last bit of evidence—what little there was, apparently—and left.

Marita, with a pair of clean jeans, sweater, and a makeup bag in hand, locked the front door behind them, despite the futility of the measure. Landon said nothing as he took her hand, led her down the steps and out to the parking lot.

She climbed in the passenger's seat of his Jeep and Landon started the engine.

"Thank you for coming to my rescue," she told him. "Thank you—so very much." Her eyes filled with tears again.

Landon backed the four-wheeler out of the parking lot and headed back toward town. As he drove, she again sniffled steadily, tears streaming down her cheeks, seemingly unable to stop.

"Why did this happen to me? Why me? I have nothing anyone would want—"

He reached out and touched her arm. "Like the officer said, it was probably nothing more than a random break-in. More than likely the burglar didn't have a clue as to what was in your apartment—or even if you owned anything of value. And when you walked in the room and startled him, he hit you and took off. If this guy had been a violent criminal he would have done much more than that. He's more than likely an amateur. A scary inconvenience for you, yes, but nothing to be frightened about."

"You don't think so?"

"No, I don't."

⇢⇥⟡⇤⇠

In a very short time, they were across town and inside Landon's apartment. Marita tried to hold back her tears, blew her nose, and took the drink Landon handed her. He wanted only to comfort her, then seek his own bed. Alone.

"It's brandy. It will help you get some rest," he said as he sat next to her on the couch.

She took a shaky sip and dabbed at her face with the tissue he had given her. "I should have never walked in the room. But I was so mad that someone had broken into my home that way...I went toward him instead of away."

Landon nodded and patted her knee reassuringly.

She glanced hard at him. "It was awful. He saw me, and he lunged. Then he was gone before I could even shout."

"All right," Landon said. "That's enough. You need to get some rest. The sun will be up in a couple of hours." He gestured to a door across the room, amending his decision about seeking his own bed. "You can sleep in the bedroom. I'll stay out here on the couch."

⇢⇥⟡⇤⇠

Landon said good night, closed the bedroom door and, she assumed, headed for the couch.

When she was alone, Marita put her makeup bag in the small adjoining bathroom and laid her clothes over the back of a chair. She stood and stared around his bedroom.

Disappointed that he hadn't wanted to sleep with her, she went to lie on his bed in the darkness, still dressed in her jeans. Tears of frustration coursed silently down her cheeks. How long had she waited to be in Landon's bed?

Never once had she imagined she would end up there alone. Alone, alone, alone—the story of her wretched life.

89

Twenty minutes later, still soaking up self-pity like a sponge, she slipped quietly from the bed, padded over to the door, eased it open and crossed the room to stand by the sofa. The silvery glow of moonlight that cascaded through the slats in the slatted blinds provided the only illumination in the room. Still, her gaze had no trouble immediately focusing on Landon's prone figure, which lay unceremoniously draped across the sofa.

She stared at the dark outlines of his face, barely visible in the thin shadows of light. A stab of pain tore through her. *Some things never change,* she thought bitterly. Returning to the bedroom she thought, *Why, Landon? Why can't you love me?*

Tripping over a stack of books on the floor, she sent them skittering like dominoes across the carpet. As she stood frozen, waiting to see if the noise had awakened him, something caught her attention. The orange vinyl cover of their high school annual.

Relieved to hear no movement from the other room, she reached down and picked up the annual. She turned on the low lamp by the bed and sat down heavily on the mattress. Flipping pages absently, she found him. There he was, resplendent in his Warrior's football uniform. All-American jock, Landon Shafer.

Time had definitely not changed him. Same dark flowing hair, same warm dark-chocolate eyes. Of course, he had needed no improvement. She traced the outline of his jaw on the photo with her fingernail, recalling the one and only encounter they had back then—

She strolled the beach, well after the sun worshipers had taken their leave. Landon stood alone, hands stuffed in the pockets of his baggy jeans, staring intently at the vast expanse of water. She wanted badly to speak to him, something she would never consider at school.

Such prospective humiliation, she simply could not risk. But here, there was no one around to jeer or taunt. If he insulted or ignored her, no one would know. This alone gave her courage.

At school she knew she was well beneath his notice, as well as that of his wealthy, snotty friends. She saw herself as a fat, ugly, nonexistent entity in a world of beauty and grace. People of her ilk were not even acknowledged by the Miller Beach crowd. Long legs, chiseled features, and perfect tans insulated them from poverty, ugliness, abuse. But not heartache, she thought, with some satisfaction.

She knew his mother had recently committed suicide. And she would offer her condolences. Finger-combing her dull, lifeless hair, she took a deep breath to steady herself, threw back her shoulders and made her approach.

"Umm." She cleared her throat but that didn't stop her from mumbling awkwardly. "Aren't you Landon Shafer? I think I've seen you at school."

He turned, very nearly losing his balance in the soft sand. She saw the startled look of utter misery on his face. It broke her heart. She certainly knew how he felt.

"Who wants to know?"

"I—I do. Ah, we have a class together."

No spark of recognition in his eyes. She wasn't surprised. "So?"

"I just wanted to say how sorry I am to hear about your mom."

He seemed to soften a bit then. "I appreciate that," he said. "What did you say your name was again?"

She could smell the booze on his breath when he shuffled from one bare foot to the other, rather unsteadily.

"Landon, have you been drinking?"

"Hell, yes! And I'm gonna drink a damned sight more, too!" He rubbed his chin thoughtfully. "Tell you what...you drive me to the liquor store and we'll have a drink together."

Both were underage, yet buying alcohol didn't pose a problem. In a bohemian paradise such as Miller Beach, everyone did pretty much as they wanted, in some regards. Especially if you were a permanent resident. So she and Landon bought their liquor and drove to North End to park at a secluded sand-bar pit.

He drank with force while she took but a sip now and then, just to be sociable. And just as she suspected, it wasn't long before the alcohol loosened his tongue and he began to talk about the pain of losing his mother. And about Caroline want-ing nothing more to do with him.

At this point this fat, ugly girl was genuinely sympathetic, was just happy she was actually alone with the most popular guy in school. But the car was like an oven and she was thank-ful when he suggested they sit on the cool bank.

Before she knew what had happened, they were in the water. He kissed her, touched her, stripped her.

She thought she must be dreaming. They went all the way, his dark, sleek body, a study in contrast to her pale, overweight one. He was sweet and kind—until the end when he reached his climax and the name he called out was not this girl's—

"Caroline, Caroline, Caroline." The sound reverberated as if it were the echo of the surf.

Bastard. He didn't even realize his mistake. He was sick and drunk. She drove him back to the beach in silence. There, without another word, she climbed back into her dad's run-down Ford Fairlane 500 and drove home, to the only slum in Miller Beach.

The Tower Trailer Court was so named because of its close proximity to the small airport. In her world, old mobile homes listed on concrete block foundations and snot-nosed kids played in postage-stamp yards. Household garbage littered the dirt path that led to her front door. She went inside, col-lapsing on her narrow bed. A jet whined—an earthquake from overhead—and the little trailer trembled until long after the plane was gone.

Monday at school, she tried to keep a low profile. As it turned out she needn't have worried. Landon Shafer didn't know she was alive anymore than he ever had.

*In fact, he never spoke to or looked at her again. Evidently
he'd been intoxicated to the point that he didn't remember a
thing. Hurt beyond words, she vowed one day to hear Landon
Shafer call her name in the throes of passion.*

―――⋇❖⋇――

Marita turned the page back to reality and located her picture in the old high school annual at the same time.

Unbelievable, she thought as she rose and entered the
adjoining bath. Stripping off her clothes, she scrutinized her
face and body's reflection in the mirror.

She smiled. Her appearance today was so altered from the
way she had looked in high school that neither Landon nor
Caroline had any clue they had ever seen her before.

Yes. She was literally quite stunning now. All those work-
outs had definitely paid off. Flat belly, firm breasts, not an
ounce of flab anywhere. A nose job, different hair color, fash-
ionable clothes—but still it hadn't been enough. Not for
Landon. Even now, he didn't want her.

A sudden rush of desperation swept through her. She knew
this was her last chance. If she couldn't get him now, she
would never get him. She had to decide what to do. Losing to
Caroline wasn't an option.

Contemplating her next move, she saw a pile of Landon's
dirty clothes in the corner. Quickly, she retrieved a shirt from
the top of the small heap. Crushing the soft cotton to her face,
she breathed in the mingled scents of his body, along with his
cologne and utter masculinity. Aroused, she slipped the shirt
on and returned to his bed where she inwardly suffered in frustration and unfulfilled desire until she fell asleep.

―――⋇❖⋇――

Marita was in the kitchen making breakfast the next morning when she heard Landon come into the room.

He looked surprisingly alert for the tired man she had said

93

good night to six hours before. He stood there, so handsome in his jeans and no shirt, with his sleep-rumpled hair and unshaven face.

She gave him a small smile and he sat at the table. Not certain of what else to say, she asked, "Care for coffee?"

"Don't mind if I do." His voice seemed unused to speaking so early in the day.

She felt him watching her closely, and a tingle began deep in the middle of her body. So did a sudden wave of warmth in her viscera.

"Thanks for the coffee," he said after a moment.

His eyes drifted slightly. He was looking at her shirt—his shirt—the one she had taken from the pile of dirty clothes last night. She could feel him looking at her hips and bare thighs. Critically. Assessingly. Even lasciviously.

A sudden rise in her chest made her breath come a bit more quickly. She could feel her nipples hardening against the material of his shirt. One glance like that from him and her insides began to melt. Pleased, she went back to the stove.

Yet she spun around to face him. "I hope you don't mind my borrowing one of your shirts to sleep in. We left my apartment so suddenly last night, I didn't think to bring anything to sleep in."

"No problem," he said quickly.

His features looked purposefully blank. *Damn him!*

He was saying, "I'm sorry I didn't offer you something to wear in the first place."

"Right." She returned to her cooking.

"You're up early this morning," he said conversationally.

"Like Caroline, I'm up at this hour every morning." She waved a spatula. "Unlike you, we have to be at the station by nine A.M., remember? That reminds me. I wonder how Caroline is this morning."

"What do you mean?"

"Nothing really." She smiled a little and stirred the scrambled eggs in the iron skillet one last time before scraping them onto two plates, then glancing at Landon.

94

The toast popped up; she buttered it. Setting a plate in front of him, she explained, "It's just that when I told her yesterday that we were going out, she wasn't in a very good mood."

"Don't you want to talk about what happened last night?"

Marita sat down across the table and immediately felt the blood rushing to her face. Why did her body always seem to play tricks on her when he was around?

She cleared her throat. "What more is there to talk about? You were there. You know what happened. It's over."

He was stirring his coffee. She watched him with fascination. He took a sip.

"You were afraid last night when I brought you here." He turned his eyes from her to look out the small window. "A break-in is a very upsetting thing to anyone, much less a woman living alone. I just thought you might feel the need to talk."

"I think I can handle it now."

"You know," he said, "you haven't told me what you're going to do."

"About the break-in?"

He nodded.

"I am going to go back to my apartment, clean it up, and go on with my life. That's what I'm going to do," she announced. "What other choice do I have?"

His eye narrowed slightly. "None, I guess."

She didn't think he would offer to have her stay with him. And he didn't.

Chapter Ten

"The coffee smells good."

Lost in thought this Monday morning, Caroline hadn't heard Sandy come into the kitchen. She turned to her friend, the same moment the housekeeper closed the back door. Standing just inside the doorway, Sandy took off her coat, ready to start work.

"Good morning." Caroline wiped her palms on a kitchen towel. "I was just about to put these cinnamon rolls into the microwave. How are you this morning?"

"Better than you, it seems. You look tired. Didn't you sleep well last night?"

Caroline walked across the room like a condemned man. She opened the microwave to pop in the plate of rolls. "Sure, I did. I just woke up early and couldn't go back to sleep, so I thought I would go ahead and start breakfast. Is that so odd?"

"You don't like to cook," Sandy reminded her.

"Does this look like I'm cooking?" Caroline slammed the door of the microwave, punched in two minutes on the timer panel and hit the start button. But nothing happened. She pressed the start button, again. Still nothing.

"This blasted microwave is not working," she muttered, turning back to her. "Sandy, it's not working again," she said. "Help."

Sandy casually draped her coat over the back of a kitchen chair and shook her head. She walked over to stand next to Caroline and nudged her out of the way. "Maybe it's that black cloud over your head that's shorting it out."

"Very funny."

Sandy opened the door of the microwave and closed it again. Without hesitation, she reset the timer and pressed the proper button. The oven roared into action.

"Smart ass," Caroline said, and went to pour two coffees.

Sandy laughed and took the cup Caroline handed her. "Oh, nice talk! Takes one to know one."

They both laughed and went to sit down at the table. Just as they did, the microwave beeped. "I'll get it," Sandy said, standing.

"Please do," Caroline said, gesturing toward the oven. "I wouldn't want it to blow up or anything."

Sandy retrieved the rolls and brought them to the table. "All right." She retook a seat. "Are you going to tell me what's wrong this morning, or not?"

Caroline gave her a sidelong glance and hesitated, balancing the pros and cons of telling her about the dreams. "Do you always have to be so nosy?"

Sandy shrugged. "I'm a small-town girl. I like to know other people's business. Do you mind?"

"I don't mind. When I mind, you'll know it."

"Well?"

Caroline mindlessly munched on a roll. "Well, what?"

"Tell me about it."

"I suppose you're going to pester me until I do—But it's nothing really. I've just been having these dreams."

Sandy finger-combed her graying hair. "I knew it! Those blasted nightmares again! You have got to forget about Wayne Nelson. That man is gone and is never coming back."

"This has nothing to do with Wayne. And I am not having nightmares—"

Disbelief was apparent. "Caroline, there's something you're not telling me. Wait. I take that back. There is a lot you're not telling me."

"All right. You win. Where would you like me to start?"

"At the beginning would be nice."

"Are you sure you want to talk about this?" Caroline asked

as if she really thought there was a chance Sandy might say no. "Now that I think about it, this could take a while."

"I work for you, remember? I have all day—"

"I don't though. Some of us have to work for a living."

Sandy glanced at the clock on the wall. "You don't have to be at the station for a full hour. Plenty of time to give me a short synopsis."

"One thing is I've been having, what I guess you could say are...erotic dreams."

"What? You're not serious!"

"I most certainly am," Caroline said softly.

Sandy drummed her fingernails on the tabletop. "And just who have you been dreaming about?"

"Just who do you think?"

"Landon? Oh, my...Does he know?"

"Hardly."

"But you're going to tell him."

"If you really think so, Sandy, then whatever drugs you're on, I want some of them!"

"Okay. I get the message, but you said that was one thing. How about telling me what else is bothering you?"

The telephone rang then and Caroline was literally saved by the bell. Relieved, she went to answer it. "Hello."

For a moment she listened, and then realized that no one had said anything on the other end of the line.

"Hello?"

She was about to hang up the receiver when she felt a cold chill shoot up her spine.

Then quite firmly the caller hung up.

"What was that?"

At the sound of Sandy's voice, a sudden warmth washed over her. "Nothing. Just a wrong number I guess. The caller hung up."

"Really? That's odd," Sandy said.

Caroline sat back down. "Why is that?"

"The same thing happened twice to me this week."

"Here or at home?"

"Here," Sandy said, matter of factly. "But I'm sure it's nothing." She paused to lean forward in a conspiratorial manner. "Anyway, you were about to tell me what else has been bothering you—"

Caroline smiled and looked at her watch. "Yes, I suppose I was, but I can't now." She stood. "It's almost time to leave for the office. I must get dressed."

"Not fair!"

"I promise to tell you later, you old gossip hound," Caroline said with a laugh and headed out of the kitchen.

Sandy yelled after her retreating figure, "If you want the linens washed today just strip the bed and leave the sheets on the floor!"

"Will do! And thanks!"

Upstairs, Caroline went straight to her closet and picked out her clothes for the day. She proceeded to the bathroom, flipped on the light, and then made her way back to the bed to strip the sheets for Sandy.

She folded the comforter covered with the white duvet neatly and set it aside, then placed the sham-covered pillows on top. Grabbing a corner of first one pillow then the other, she snatched the cases off and tossed them to the floor. Next she grabbed the top sheet and pulled it away from the fitted one. As she did, a something long and skinny fell to the floor.

She screamed. "Ohmigod!"

A small snake with multicolor bands quickly slithered off into the bathroom.

Caroline shot forward and slammed the door behind her.

When Sandy arrived, huffing and puffing from her sprint up the stairs, Caroline was against the bathroom door, trembling.

"W—what in blue blazes—"

"A snake! It's a damn snake! A sn—snake was in the sheets! And it's in the bathroom now!"

"What kind of snake?" Sandy asked.

"Blast and blazes! How should I know?" Caroline screamed. "I wasn't about to stop his forward slithering to ask."

Sandy placed hands on her hips. "What I meant was—what did it look like?"

"I don't know! Multicolored, banded, small...beyond that I have no idea!"

Sandy rubbed her chin. "Hmm—"

"Hmm? What the devil is that supposed to mean?"

"It sounds like a coral snake to me. And those guys are b-b-b-bad boys, let me tell you. It doesn't take long to die after you get bitten by one of those babies." She waved a hand. "Here, move so I can get a peek—"

Caroline stiffened and flatted both palms loudly against the door. "Are you high? I am not moving one inch until you call 'snake away!'"

Sandy sighed expansively. "Then you had better stuff a sheet under the door to block that big crack—"

"Oh, no!" Caroline propelled herself off the door and out of the room.

That was the last time she would ever get into bed without shaking out the sheets first!

An hour and a half later, Caroline was still in no shape to drive to the office, so Sandy volunteered to drive her in the Jag. No Volkswagen followed as they rode to Magic 97. Thank heavens. That would have been all she needed.

Still, Caroline shivered. She shifted her position in the seat and looked over at Sandy. "You don't think I could have slept with that—that thing all night, do you?"

"Who knows? Snakes of any sort, including coral snakes, don't generally attack without some type of provocation." Sandy made a left turn at the light. "But I doubt he was out to get you. More than likely the snake came in during the night sometime—sort of like 'a little lamb who'd lost its way.'"

"Cute." Caroline sat back and crossed her arms over her chest.

Sandy cleared her throat to keep from laughing. "I'm sorry. I was just kidding. Things were getting entirely too serious."

"I'll have you know that I find nothing about this—" a wild gesturing of hands "—this thing that happened to me as funny in the least."

"No, I don't suppose you would," Sandy said with exaggerated seriousness. "Personally, I'm just thankful you aren't a reckless sleeper. 'Cause if you were one to toss and turn a lot in your sleep, or kicked the covers and such, you might very well be dead now."

Caroline threw her hands up. "Well, thank you, Mr. Fowler. If I had wanted to know the details, I would have simply tuned in to the *Wild Creatures of Nature* on Sunday night!"

By the time they pulled the Jag into Magic 97's parking lot, the daytime crew had already arrived at work.

With Sandy in tow carrying papers for her, Caroline walked into the station that morning and made a concentrated effort to appear absolutely composed and normal in spite of all the mental unrest she had been forced to endure lately.

"Well, I'll be," Sandy said as she stopped her forward motion. "I haven't seen you for ages. Mary Jo Taylor, don't you look wonderful."

Mary Jo Taylor?

Sandy glanced at Caroline. "I didn't know you had someone that went to high school with you working here."

Neither did I, Caroline thought, *until now.* But Sandy had called the receptionist "Mary Jo."

Marita stood fidgeting behind her desk. "Nice to see you again, Ms. Sandy."

Caroline gave her a sideways glance. "I thought your name was Marita Taubold. That is the name on the checks I sign, isn't it?" she asked, then peered at an obviously confused Sandy.

"Yes, of course," Marita said, drawing her attention again. "You see, as Ms. Sandy said, I have changed a good bit since we went to high school and...and well, I changed my name, too."

"But why?" Caroline asked, genuinely curious.

If she were the one who had changed that much for the better, she would have shouted it to the world—not changed her name and tried to hide the fact.

Still, although she did not remember "Mary Jo," that made her feel bad. Had she been that wrapped up in her own little clique when she was in high school that she wouldn't remember a classmate? Surely, she hadn't been that conceited. At least she hoped not—

"Let's just say I wasn't very popular in school and when I moved away and changed, I changed everything," said Marita or whoever she was. "I moved back to Miller Beach last year, a totally different person. No one, until now that is, even noticed I lived here before. Or that I'd changed my name. So, I never felt the need to say anything. That's all. I hope it's not a problem."

"No, of course not," Caroline said. "Why should it be? That's your business, not anyone else's."

Marita smiled a little, but before she could comment Sandy chimed in, "I think 'Marita' fits you. A very good choice, if I do say so. You don't look anything like a 'Mary Jo' anymore."

Caroline cleared her throat. "I'm already late this morning and I need to get to work. If you'll excuse us, M—Marita—"

She smiled. "Certainly."

In her office, Caroline put down her briefcase on her desk and turned to take the stack of papers from Sandy. "Will you pick me up at five?"

Sandy crossed her heart and pretended to spit. "On the dot."

Caroline laughed. "'Bye."

She also narrowly averted a minor stroke when she turned around and saw yet another faxed copy of a sinister-looking newspaper article sticking up out of her machine. Just as with the others—no source, no date, just a bold headline:

SOCIETY WIFE SHOT BY HUSBAND'S MISTRESS   NO ARREST
MADE

Snatching the fax, she sat at her desk. Rubbing her neck
and her temples, Caroline read it quickly, then crumpled it up
and tossed the fax in the trash. Enough was enough. Maybe it
was time to tell the authorities.

But what would she tell them? That she had been receiv-
ing faxed copies of reprinted Associated Press articles over her
office fax? Right! With her luck, the police would think she
was the nut—not the person who sent a radio station an occa-
sional copy of nationally printed newspaper article.

Caroline jumped at the sound of the intercom, then
punched the lighted button with force. "What is it, Marita?"

"There's a man out here to see you."

"I don't have any appointments this morning. Who is he
and what does he want?"

"I don't know, Caroline. But he said it's personal."

"Fine. Send him back." Dammit—now she was saying
fine!

At the knock on her office door, she looked up to see none
other than Wayne Nelson in the flesh.

Caroline straightened her spine and crossed her arms over
her chest. "To what do I owe this horror—oh, sorry. I mean
honor, Mr. Nelson?"

Her ex-husband held his hands up in mock surrender.
"Hey, Caroline. I was just in town on business and thought I'd
drop by and see how life was treating my wife," he offered.
"Judging by the warmth of your greeting, I would have to say
not very damn well."

"Firstly, I am *not* your wife any longer. Secondly, what do
you want, Wayne? In case you haven't noticed, I have a business of my own to run."

"I'm after a truce. I'm sorry to hear about Sheldon's death.
My intention was to offer condolences and see if there's any-

thing I could do to help. I know how close you were." He paused to shift his weight from one booted foot to the other. "Besides, I've really missed you since I've been gone," he finally admitted.

"You should have considered that possibility before you asked for a divorce. As it stands, I really don't give a good damn."

Suddenly, all the anger, all the frustration and fright of the past weeks crystallized in an instant.

When Caroline caught sight of the crumpled fax in the wastebasket, a current of enlightenment rushed through her brain. Faxes. Wayne. Phone calls. Wayne. Being followed. Wayne.

All Wayne!

"You bastard! Truce my ass!" She grabbed the paper from the refuse can, and came from behind her desk and shoved it directly under his nose. "You did this! How dare you! What did you think? That if I were frightened enough I would sell the station and run home to bake cookies and be your brood mare?"

Before he had a chance to defend himself, Caroline threw the document down and huffed back to her desk, plopping into her chair.

"Caroline, I honestly don't know what in the hell you are talking about. Have you completely lost your mind?"

"Lost my mind? Ha! To my knowledge, the only time I have ever taken leave of my senses was the day I married you, Wayne Nelson." Her voice reverberated through the room. "And unless you want to find yourself in a whole heap of trouble, you had better stop harassing me. Now, get the hell out of my office!"

Wayne hesitated a second longer than her frazzled nerves could bear. The Waterford crystal paperweight on her desk, a wedding gift no less, exploded against the door the instant he closed it behind him.

Bet he isn't laughing now!

Caroline paced back and forth across the room, ran her fingers through her hair, chewed on a thumbnail. She looked at her watch and wished Sandy would hurry up and arrive. She couldn't stand still. Her breathing became so shallow and rapid, she thought she just might need a paper bag to keep from hyperventilating.

Could this be an anxiety attack?

Adrenaline propelled her to the treadmill by the window. After several minutes of concentrated exercise, Caroline heard a car door slam and looked out the window in the nick of time to see Marita hop happily into Landon's Cherokee.

Just great! Make my day, why don't you? She ceremoniously raised her index finger to her temple and fired.

Suddenly overwhelmed, Caroline dropped into her desk chair and put her face in her hands. Why did Marita being with Landon bother her so much? She wasn't interested in him anyway.

Then a little voice asked her, *If you're not interested in him, why are you so angry?*

—◦◦◦◦◦—

Damned if he wasn't as tired as a one-armed paperhanger.

"Hey, Landon. Get the lead out! It's three minutes 'til midnight and the call-board is already lit up like a Christmas tree," Mike said from the control room. "It's time to get this show on the road!"

Landon nodded and put on his headphones. When he pointed to Mike, he flipped a switch that gave him an on-air drumroll, reminiscent of a popular song of staccato percussions.

The On-Air light illuminated above Landon's door and then Mike announced in his tight-fisted Alabama accent, "Ladies and gentlemen, here comes Landon Shafer and 'Sinful Secrets!'"

Two seconds later, Mike pointed to him and mouthed, "You're on."

"Thank you very much," Landon said in his best Elvis imitation, which wasn't very good at all.

Via the control board, canned applause, cheers, then whistles chimed in.

"Good midnight, Miller Beach. I'm Landon Shafer and this is 'Sinful Secrets.'"

More canned applause.

Landon took a deep breath. "Here's your chance to share your utmost sexual fantasies every weeknight from midnight 'til two. The number to call, 555-FANTASY, and we've got our first caller. Hi, you're on the air with Landon Shafer and 'Sinful Secrets.'"

"Hello," said a woman who sounded exactly like Mae West. So much, Landon waited for her to say, "Why don't you come up and see me sometime—?"

"Hello, right back atcha sexy lady. Do you have a fantasy or sinful secret you'd like to share with us?"

"I sure do. The question is—would you like to hear it?"

"Ooh baby, ooh baby, ooh!" Landon piped in and looked at his producer. "Hey, Mike. I think it's going to be a hot time in the old town tonight!"

The caller giggled. "Are you ready?"

"Is a frog's butt watertight?"

"All right, here goes—" She took a deep breath. "I'm shopping in this mall when I see this great-looking guy coming toward me. We make eye contact, and through some well-practiced body language I indicated I'd like it if he followed me—"

"Does he?" Landon asked.

"Oh yes," she said. "And a lot more—"

"Please go on."

"Well, I walk around the mall for a while longer, making him wait, and then I go into this kind of restaurant. It's like an old diner type of place and has tables, a horseshoe-shaped counter and a booth where you can have you pictures taken."

"One of those things you step in, sit on a stool and close a curtain?"

"That's it. How did you know?"

Landon cocked an eyebrow at Mike. "Just a lucky guess."

"Anyway," she said, "I go over to this machine and put a dollar in the slot. Then I go inside the booth and wait for him to follow me. Of course he does, and he closes the curtain behind him. And this machine takes pictures while we...do it."

"Caller, that was fantastic!" Landon threw up his hands. "Mike, was that a great fantasy or what?"

"Man, the word hardly describes it. You know, I'm not sure the next caller will even come close."

"There's only one way to find out. Throw me that next caller!"

"You bet. Landon, we have our old friend 'Kitten' on line two. If she can't top the last caller, I don't know who can."

For some ungodly reason an old high school cheer came to Landon's mind: *Kitten, Kitten, she's our man. If she can't do it, no one can!*

Okay, so maybe he gotten even more tired than he'd thought—

He shook his head to clear it and punched line two. "Hi, Kitten. You're on the air. How the hell are you?"

"Purr-fect."

Landon laughed. "Now, that was a good one."

"Yep," Mike cut in from the control room. "She is da cat-woh-man."

"Oh, Mike," Landon said, waving a hand in front of his nose. "That was bad, man. I always knew there was a reason why you are in the control room and not on the air."

"Hey, Kitten. You still with us?"

"Yes." She hesitated. "I'm here."

"Please tell us your fantasy for the night. I know I can speak for all the listeners out there when I say, we can hardly wait!"

"Here goes then. You see, there's this guy I know—one that I am very attracted to—"

"And?" Landon prompted.

"And, well...he doesn't know. At least not the true extent of my attraction. Anyway, one night, due to circumstances beyond our control, of course, I end up having to spend the night at his house."

"Of course."

"But it's not what you're thinking."

"It's not?"

"No," she said. "We don't end up sleeping in the same room. He gives me his bedroom, then he goes out to sleep on the couch."

Mike said, "Low blow. The Bummer man delivers—"

Landon thought, *No, it can't be.* "Ah...what happens then, Kitten?"

"He falls asleep. And when he does, I get up and sneak out to the living room to look at him."

Landon swallowed. "Just look?"

She laughed, deep and throaty. "For now. I even go back into the bedroom, after I get my fill. If you know what I mean."

Landon began to perspire. He took a sip of coffee from his cup. "Yes, I—I suppose I do—"

"Then I run my fingers over everything in his bedroom, his books, his bed linens, his furniture—touching, caressing. I open his closet and run my hands through his clothes, press my face to them, inhale his scent. And I become...shall we say, excited."

Landon remained quiet. Mike raised an eyebrow, imparting a sidelong glance from the control room.

"And since I can't have him live and in person, I figure the next best thing is to undress and put on one of his shirts, so that I can pretend he is with me—"

Again, Landon swallowed. Hard.

"I take one of his dress shirts and pull it on, but I don't button it. I close my eyes and pretend my hands are his, and that his fingers are fondling my breasts, my nipples—" She began to breathe heavily into the phone. As if she wasn't merely telling her fantasy.

Landon adjusted his seat in the chair, leaned forward, and rested his forearms on the tabletop.

"He touches me, traces a path down my stomach until he begins—" She paused and she took several short intakes of breath. Then, "Oh...oh!"

Landon lunged forward, which sent his coffee cup across flying across the desk and CDs tumbling in rapid-fire succession everywhere. But he did manage to hit his intended button, cutting her off.

"Beeeeeeep! This is a test. This is only a test of your emergency broadcasting system. If there was an emergency in your area you would be instructed—"

Mike jumped from his chair, jerked open the door and shot out of the control room. "Boy, was that quick thinkin', big guy!"

Landon shoved a hand through his hair, taking his headphones off at the same time. "Where the hell were you? It's your job to—to stop something like that! Not mine!"

Mike raised his hands, palm up. "I was just getting ready to—"

"Never mind! I don't want to know! Get back in there and punch in a commercial set!"

Mike spun around while Landon slammed his hand down in a puddle of coffee. *Shit!*

Now he had real trouble and it wasn't the kind that would go away unless he did something drastic.

Chapter Eleven

It was late, literally and figuratively, but not too late. Once Landon's mind was made up, his long legs pumped to the parking lot, his Cherokee. Within five minutes, he was headed down Lake Shore Drive toward Caroline's.

Once there, he cautiously opened the front door with the key he had been given by Caroline's father so many years ago and stepped inside. Soft moonlight lighted the living room through the large picture window as he made his way on silent footsteps up the staircase.

Deep breathing greeted his own labored, uneven breath as he eased open her bedroom door. He forced himself to a calmness that he didn't feel. She couldn't be, but she was, sound asleep. Unsettled that she hadn't heard him, he could have been anyone, a burglar, a madman, a—a—No! He refused to think of it. If he hadn't had a key, she would have heard the intruder. Surely.

He stood for a moment, undecided. Should he wake her? Should he approach her as he yearned to, then bend down and kiss her gently on the mouth hoping to wake her?

In the soft moonlight, he noticed that Caroline was sleeping in his old high school football jersey. He could clearly see the large white numbers "87" across her chest. The thought pleased him when he thought of how she had fought tooth and nail to get it from him.

Did she feel what he was feeling? Did she want him as much as he wanted her?

She must.

He knew Caroline sensed rather than saw his approach to the bed, as well as the slight movement of his body when he knelt on his knees.

She screamed, slapping a hand to her chest and shooting upward in bed. "How did you get in here?"

He smiled sheepishly. "The key."

"What key?"

He dangled the gold chain in front of her. "The key that was given to me by your father when my mother and I moved in here."

Her jaw dropped. "You still have that?"

"Obviously."

"Well, give it back!" She moved to snatch the key from his hand, but he was too fast.

She swatted at him again but Landon held it out of her reach. "Ah-ah-ah. This belongs to me."

"It doesn't anymore! Give it to me or I'll—"

"Or, you'll what?" He laughed. "You and whose army are going to take it from me?"

He could see she forced herself to relax, making her breaths slow and even.

Caroline then crossed her arms defiantly over her chest. "What is it you want from me in the middle of the night?"

"To talk to you," he said honestly. He realized the words he spoke so defensively were true. He did want to talk with her, to talk about Marita—to make things right between them. He swallowed hard and waited for her to answer.

"So you can tell me all about your new love affair?"

"I am not having a love affair with Marita."

"Really? So you've never slept with her?"

He was about to say, "Technically, no," but decided quickly that it was far better not to confirm or deny that loaded question.

Instead, he waggled a finger back and forth. "Sex and a love affair are not the same thing."

"*Touché*. Of all women, I should know that's how you feel, shouldn't I?"

"That wasn't necessary. You're the one who ended things between us, not me."

Now she was the one to refuse to confirm anything. "I really have nothing to say to you, Landon. So why don't you just leave the way you came? And don't let the door hit you in the butt on the way out."

"Why do you have to be so mean, Caroline? Why won't you just listen to me?"

She raised her hand and pounded on her chest. "Because you hurt me here!"

That was all it took. Her verbal attack had made him angry, unreasonably so, he realized, but angry nonetheless. He had done nothing to cause her this pain, which she seemed to think he had deliberately inflicted.

He rose from his knees and threw her against the bed, his body atop hers, intent on getting her to listen to him. "And you think you didn't hurt me?"

"Let go of me," she demanded, heaving his weight, attempting to slide out from beneath him. "Go back to Marita! Go back and take what you want from her! You won't find me so stupidly willing to share your bed again!" Glistening tears welled in her bright blue eyes. There was just enough moonlight spilling thorough the bedroom window curtain to see them sparkling on her long lashes.

Landon looked at her incredulously. In the semidarkness he had never seen her look more beautiful. Her hair gleamed with silver belonging to the moon alone; her skin had a glowing smoothness, was softer and sleeker than any other woman he had ever known.

At his touch on her cheek, she leaned her face into his hand, her eyes closing, her lips parting.

Wordlessly, he smoothed these light golden waves, feeling the satiny strands between his fingers, thinking that her hair was like the moon itself, shining and sleek.

When she turned to him, it was as if she didn't know what to say.

His gaze remained steady. "It was one day in July, when

112

you were seventeen," he whispered. "It was hot, blistering hot, when I saw you swimming in that skimpy bikini in the ocean. I wanted you, and thought about jumping in the water with you. Then I thought that all the other guys on the beach probably saw you the same way I did, and had the same thoughts about you I did. I wanted to shake you until your perfectly white teeth rattled. You know what happened that evening?" he continued softly. "While I was making love to you in that stifling boathouse, the sweat was running down my back, but I didn't think of anything but you that day. All I could think of was the way you had turned so sweet and wild in my arms, lying under me and burning me with a different kind of heat. I never minded the suffocating summer heat after that day, because all I had to do was look up at that Georgia sun and I thought of making love to you."

He kissed her softly, on the cheek.

Caroline swallowed, seemed unable to speak or move.

"Someone once said a great romance begins with a look, a kiss, a whispered promise in the dark—I promise to do things right this time, if you'll only give me the chance. Let me make love to you again, now."

"Please," she said, and wrapped her arms around his neck. "Please make love to me."

He stood, took off his shirt, before lifting the covers and climbing in bed beside her. He tugged his old football jersey over her head and settled over her, with her breasts pressed against his chest. She sucked in her breath at the same moment he did.

"This is so much nicer than fighting, when you're snappin' like a damned catfish," he said, and kissed her even as he rubbed himself against her.

"You feel wonderful, too, Landon."

"And you feel soft and warm, like silk slowly rubbing against my flesh."

She opened her mouth and he gave her his tongue. His tongue entered her mouth at the same time his hand moved, flat and smooth over her belly to remove her panties. Then he returned his fingers to curve around her waist.

His fingers rested there, not moving, just touching her to feel the heat of her and for her to feel the heat of him. Then he merely pressed down, giving her the weight of his hand against her flesh. She quivered; he felt it. And he exhaled a sigh of relief. He was also harder than stone. It was unnerving, nearly painful, and it drove him insane.

Caroline looked when Landon kissed her and raised his body enough to remove his jeans. His eyes were closed and his thick black lashes lay against his lean cheeks. He was utterly beautiful, and this was what she wanted, what she'd wanted every day of her life since that night in the boathouse—when she knew she loved him with all her heart—would always love him.

Ah, his strong hands and fingers resting again on the firm mound just below her belly, staying there, lightly pressing against her, and it felt right for him to be there with her. Then he opened his eyes.

He reached out slowly to touch her hair. "You are so beautiful."

She smiled although her stomach felt the way it had once, long ago, when she'd raced across the water in a runaway sailboat. Speaking softly, her words interspersed with soft sighs, she told him how much she had missed him and how sorry she was that they had wasted so many years. Landon shifted so that he straddled her hips, nothing threatening in the motion.

Caroline trembled, even as strange, remembered heat began pulsating deep within her, making her breasts rise and fall under Landon's dark gaze. He bent and licked the sensitive skin between her breasts and the woodsy scent of his cologne wafted to her.

By the time his tongue had traced a moist path to her hardened nipple, Caroline well knew the heated desperation. With her back arched, she tangled her fingers in Landon's abundant hair, trying to guide him to the sustenance she needed so badly to give.

He took the covers away, then drew her right knee up and wide of her left. With measured strokes, he teased that moist junction already prepared for him.

"Listen to me," he grated out, grasping her chin in his hand. "No woman has ever possessed my heart and soul but you, Caroline Hunt, and I am going to make love to you like you have never been made love to before. If you have any objections, you'd better speak up now, while I've still got enough control to stop myself."

She bit her lower lip, just in case her pride rose and saved her from what her body so desperately craved.

"All right then, my sweet," Landon said in a tone of gentle finality. And he took up where he left off in the slow dance of love.

She gave a whimper when he took a thick lock of her hair and brushed each nipple with it. She stretched her arms above her head and gripped the headboard of the bed, lying before him, an offering for the taking.

The lush woodsy smell of him rose to engulf her again, and she closed her eyes to savor the pleasure.

He rolled a nipple between index finger and thumb until Caroline, remembering that pleasure very well, begged him in a breathless gasp to take it into his mouth. He did so without hesitation, greedily and lustily, and the hand that had held her lock of hair shifted to lift her hips.

"Put your arms around my neck," he coaxed.

She did as told, burying her face in the matted hair of his chest; his hand caressed her. She groaned as sensation after sensation rippled through her in time to the alluring movements of his fingers. She sipped at his soft full lips.

His lips fused with hers, melding their mouths together and sealing them with heat. His tongue eased along the inside of her lips.

"Do that to me," he said urgently.

She did and was rewarded with an animal growl deep from

his throat. When next their mouths came together, her tongue darted into his mouth. A fleeting flirtation that seemed to excite him even more.

"Caroline, sweet Caroline. You are so wonderful."

His lips found her ear and blessed it with ardent attention. Strong teeth worried her earlobe. When his tongue had soothed her flesh, his lips dried it.

"Please, Landon," she said, turning her head toward his mouth. He seemed to know her request before she asked it. He licked at her lips with slow, leisurely strokes. "That feels so wonderful."

She pressed her breasts against the crinkly down tufts on his chest. It tickled and teased her nipples until they ached again for a firmer touch. She plumped them with her own hands and pushed against the hardness that was his chest, finding the counterparts of his nipples. She rubbed them roughly with her own.

A sharp cry escaped his surprised lips and he crushed her to him. His mouth started an uncharted trail down her chest to her breasts. His tongue beat against her nipples like the kiss of a butterfly. Then one was enveloped in his mouth. She believed he drew her very soul into his and she gave it freely, with great pleasure.

The pulsing action of his mouth echoed the throbbing in the lower part of her body. As though on cue, his hand slipped between her thighs. Fingers gentle and knowing caressed, stroked, sought, and performed with such accuracy that Caroline heard her own gasps as those of a drowning woman.

Her hand slipped down his side to find his naked hip. Unconsciously, her fingers gripped him and pulled him ever closer to that part of her that silently cried out for him in wanting. "Love me, Landon."

"I am," he whispered as he stubbornly continued the slow hurtful pleasure and continued to explore the private trails and passages that held the secrets of her body. "Don't you feel me loving you?"

The blissful torture went on and on until she feared he

would never allow her release. That he would continue to hold her forever in his fine sensual prison from which she could see no escape.

Only when she clung to him with silent sobbing, and her body undulated frantically with the need to be fulfilled, did he shift his weight into position and introduce himself into her body with tentative probing.

"I've wanted this for so long, ached to be with you," he admitted.

She lay very still. Her longings rampant, her body ached to be joined completely with his. She felt herself opening to him more and more.

Finally, when she thought she would surely die if he did not give her release, he moved his body farther into hers, parting her legs wider with his own. He had an enormous erection, but she was more than ready for him; he slid into her, thrusting deeply.

She panted, moving against him, matching his rhythm, floating with him somewhere she had never been before.

Higher and higher, she rose as he moved deeper and deeper into her, and the waves of ecstasy started, began to engulf her.

She could feel him touching the very core of her with the core of himself. He was strong and hard inside her, riding the crest of her climax with her. This was the way it was meant to be. The way it should always be and never had been for her. Until Landon.

Rising higher and higher, she moaned his name over and over. He let himself go, crested with her, gave himself up to her, flowed with her and into her. And when he did, he shouted, "Oh Caroline! My sweet, sweet Caroline!"

—❖—

The sight of the black Jeep Cherokee parked in Caroline's driveway alerted the driver of the Volkswagen to the fact, *I'm not alone.* In fact, the owner, Landon Shafer, was inside, his body most definitely in that bitch's bed.

As the VW pulled away, the small headlights never once gleamed on the road until the vehicle was at least three blocks away.

Chapter Twelve

Day dawned sunny and brisk. Landon woke excited and expectant after little more than three hours sleep.

His gaze focused on Caroline where she lay sleeping next to him. Looking at her that way, so beautifully rumpled in the bed, he could easily push the problem to the back of his mind—but he wouldn't. Not again. He could no longer afford to put it off.

This thing with Marita really was a helluva mess. And he supposed he had no one to blame but himself for the current condition of his private life.

He couldn't delay the confrontation any longer. He would have a long-overdue discussion with Marita today.

He also needed to talk to Caroline. She had a right to know what Marita was doing, what he felt had turned into an obsession for her.

Of course, he had meant to speak to Caroline about everything last night, had intended to tell her that he felt certain the call-in Kitten was actually Marita. But things had simply gotten out of hand. In a good way, most definitely; he couldn't complain. Nonetheless, his train of thought had been diverted.

First things first. He must wake Caroline, then go and confront Marita. What a dummy he had been not to spot her attention for what it was. He would have thought he'd taken enough psychology classes in college to recognize an obsessive personality when he saw one.

Apparently not.

Well, I'm burnin' daylight—

"Caroline?" He kissed her lightly on the mouth.

Although her eyes remained closed she raised her arms, stretched, and then wrapped them about his neck. "Mmm?"

"You need to open your eyes." He paused to kiss both her eyelids. "We need to talk. Now, open your peepers."

She opened one eye and stuck her tongue out, briefly. "Do we have to? I was sleeping so peacefully—"

He laughed. "Yes, we have to. It's important. Sit up," he said and kissed her on the nose.

"Only because I have to." She wiggled into a sitting position.

Landon shifted his position until he was sitting with his back resting against the headboard and his arm draped around Caroline's lithe shoulders. "And I will tell you only because I have to."

She ran her hand through her sleep-rumpled hair, fluffed it, and smiled. "Okay. What's so important?"

"I don't know how I should say this, so I am just going to say it. I think we have a problem with Marita."

"What do you mean?"

He expelled an expansive sigh and told her everything. About the dates, about the break-in, about Kitten.

Although Caroline did not react in the manner Landon had thought she would—she did react.

She shook her head. "Now that we are bearing our souls, so to speak, I need to talk to you about something else."

He kissed her and pulled her back into his embrace. "Then shoot."

She ran her fingers up and down his forearm. "I've been getting these really strange faxes lately."

"Exactly what kind of faxes?"

She shrugged. "That's just it. I'm not really sure they are anything. Several times, I've gotten one at the office, from person or persons unknown. Each one is almost identical. At least the nature of the faxes is identical. All have been related to women, particularly women in some sort of peril."

"Are you saying these faxes are some sort of veiled

threats?"

"I'm saying it's possible. And then yesterday afternoon, out of the blue, Wayne shows up."

Landon narrowed his eyes. "Wayne Nelson?"

"In the flesh."

"And just what the hell did he want?"

Caroline picked at a loose thread on the hem of the sheet. "I'm not sure he wanted anything, other than to stop by and see me. Although at the time, I accused him of being the one following me all around town in that damned VW Bug. And of sending the faxes."

Landon's spine shot erect. He turned and grabbed Caroline by the shoulders. "What VW? He's been following you?"

She raised her sky-blue gaze to his. "I don't know who's been following me for sure, but someone has. Or, at least, was. I haven't seen the beige VW for a few days. I suppose there's always the possibility I could have imagined the whole thing. In any beach town there are lots of VW Bugs. Oh, Landon. I'm so confused that I'm not sure of anything anymore."

"Yes, there are a lot of old Volkswagens around here. Like all the stuff from the sixties and seventies, the Bugs have become quite popular again. Still, maybe you are being followed. And just maybe it wasn't Wayne at all. It could have been Marita."

Caroline's jaw dropped. "Marita? Does she have a car like that? A beige one?"

"Honestly, I don't know. Now that I think about it, I've never seen the car she drives. Have you?"

Caroline shook her head. "I can't say that I have."

She started gnawing on her thumbnail, apparently debating something with herself.

He decided to keep his mouth shut and give her some time to digest everything.

"Marita was just someone to occupy my time," he said finally, in a low voice. "She was never anything to me other than a friend, someone to take to dinner. Once. But if she was obsessed enough to call in to my show, pretending to be someone else, I think she could be obsessed enough to do just about anything."

"Why would she go after me, Landon?"

"Jealousy, I suppose."

"I don't know—"

"I admit, jealousy might not be a big enough reason," he said. "But it's definitely a place to start. I think it's something we should think about. I mean, I know he's a festering nob but—you don't really think Wayne is capable of something like this, do you?"

Her gaze came up. "I haven't made up my mind on that yet. But, yes, before you told me about this Marita thing, I thought so." She inhaled a deep quaff of air. "There's something else maybe we should consider—Marita's real name isn't Marita."

"It's not?" He cocked an eyebrow. "Are you going to elaborate?"

"Truthfully, I would never have known if Sandy hadn't recognized her."

Landon gave a growl of frustration. "Recognized her from what? Be specific!"

"Sandy gave me a ride to the office, and she came in the station. That's when she recognized Marita. Only not as Marita, as Mary Jo something or other."

"Mary Jo? What fresh hell is this?"

"It seems she went to high school with us, but she looked totally different then."

"Different, how?"

"I'm not really sure. Apparently, when she moved away from here she lost a good amount of weight, et cetera. Then when she decided to move back, she changed her name—I thought about looking for a 'Mary Jo' in one of our old annuals, but honestly don't think I even have one anymore."

"I do," Landon said. "I'm sure of it. When I get home I'll hunt it up."

Suddenly a door slammed downstairs. "Morning! I'm here!"

"Sandy." Caroline jumped out of bed and frantically pulled the old football jersey over her head. She bent down to snatch his jeans from the floor to hit him with them.

Yanking them away from his face, he said, "What the hell are you doing?"

Caroline began to pace, back and forth, back and forth. "Get up. Get dressed. Hurry! Sandy. It's Sandy! Oh…I forgot all about her. Oh, what's she going to say?"

Landon swung his legs over the side of the bed and pulled his jeans on. "About what?"

Caroline stopped her forward motion and planted her hands on her hips. "About you being here with me in my house, in my bed, for heaven's sake—What do you think?"

"Well, what do you know?" Sandy said from the open doorway. "Landon Shafer, as I live and breath!"

Caroline cringed, then slowly turned to see Sandy standing in the doorway with a big smile on her face. *Great, just great.*

"You have truly restored my faith," Sandy said. "Yes, you have. Now I know that dreams really can become reality!"

Landon looked first at Sandy. "What are you talking about?" When she made no comment, he then looked to Caroline. "What is she talking about?"

Caroline cast her employee-pal a damning glance. *If one more thing comes out of your mouth—* "I have no idea."

Sandy cleared her throat. "I'd best go down and start the coffee. It was good to see you again, Landon."

"Same here," he said, and she left.

As soon as the door shut behind her, Caroline gave a frustrated groan and headed for the bathroom. She dressed and waited until Landon finished his shower, before going down to breakfast.

Thankfully, Sandy made no more comments, at least for now. But as they all drank coffee and ate toast, Sandy did explain she'd had to catch a ride to work, given that her car would not start that morning. Thus, Caroline decided to leave her the Jag and caught a ride to the office with Landon.

At the station she went to get out of the Cherokee, but Landon stopped her with a hand on her arm. "Last night was really wonderful. Something straight out of a dream."

Caroline dropped her gaze. "Yes, it was," she said.

He leaned over and kissed her. "I'll be back to pick you up around five?"

She nodded and went into Magic 97.

Landon headed straight for Marita's. He'd have to hurry in order to catch her before she left for work.

Considering the amount of sleep he'd had in the last couple of days, he should have been exhausted. Why he wasn't, he had no idea. He supposed it was adrenaline running in overdrive.

It was just after eight when Landon pulled into the apartment complex's parking lot. He looked around for any sight of a beige Volkswagen Bug. There was none.

He rang the bell. With her head wrapped in a towel, Marita opened the door. She looked drawn, dark lines etched under her eyes. Her makeup was subtle, or unfinished, and seemed to emphasize her obvious lack of sleep.

"Hello, Landon. To what do I owe this honor?" She stared at the floor as if consulting some inner voice. Her manner seemed very flat.

"We need to talk."

She looked up then and cinched the belt of her robe tighter. "Now?"

"Now." He brushed past her and went into her living room.

She took a deep breath, closed the door, and followed him. Seeming to force polite behavior, she gave a thin smile. "I have to dress for work."

"This won't take long."

"All right." She sat on the chair, folded her hands in her

lap, and stared at him as if waiting for the punch line.

He looked directly at her. "First, I think it's only fair to tell you I have someone in my life now. And you and I seeing each other is something that won't happen again."

"I see," she said, straightening her spine. "May I ask who this person is?"

Although certain she already knew the answer to that question, he answered, "Caroline."

"I guess you felt a great need to re-establish a bygone relationship."

He kept his eyes trained on Marita. "Bygone relationship?"

She laughed, not a cheerful sound. "You think I don't know—that everyone doesn't know—about you and Caroline in high school?"

"That brings up another issue."

Her eyes turned a shade darker. "Such as—?"

He released a long breath. "I've just learned that you went to the same high school we did. But I cannot place you back then. Your name was Mary Jo, I've been told."

His gaze swung to hers. Her anger surged to the forefront when she rose to meet his challenge. "No, you wouldn't remember someone like me. My name was Mary Jo Taylor to be exact. But I am not that person any longer."

"I didn't realize someone could just decide to become another person."

"Obviously, one can. I did."

Landon paced. This was not what he'd come here to discuss. He waved a dismissive hand, but stopped and turned back to face her. "I'm here to discuss something else entirely."

She folded her arms. "Then what did you come here for, that is, besides to tell me that your romantic interest lies elsewhere?"

"Let me get straight to the point. Caroline is being followed and she's received threatening faxes."

"So?"

Landon took a step toward Marita. "So just what in the hell

do you think you're doing?"

Marita actually looked as if she were shocked. And he could almost believe she was innocent. "Landon, why are you saying this has anything to do with me?"

Now she looked hurt. He wasn't about to buy it.

As if she knew what he was thinking, her expression changed. "Why would I do such things?"

Landon shoved fingers through his hair . "I really don't know—jealousy, desperation? Anyone who is desperate enough to change her image and her name might do anything. Cut the bull, Marita. I know you're Kitten. What kind of sick games are you playing?"

She glanced at him with apparent discomfort. "Kitten? Who or what is Kitten? I don't know what you're talking about."

Landon laughed. "And you think I'm going to believe that?"

"I really don't give a good damn what you believe! What I can't figure out is why you are so interested in Caroline all of a sudden. Last I heard, you were angry at her over the way she treated you about the show." A rather smug look came over the receptionist's face. "Has sleeping with her once again blinded you completely?"

"That sure as hell is none of your business."

"Oh, I see—"

"Don't change the subject, Marita. We were talking about you. Not Caroline."

"About me following Caroline? You act as if I'm some jealous spouse you've dumped, or something. Don't flatter yourself. You're not that important to me. I assure you."

Suddenly he leaned forward. "Maybe," he said with forced calm. "And maybe I've known enough women like you to know how their minds work when they turn vindictive for some supposed wrong."

"Will you just take a hike?" she demanded.

"Gladly. But if you're the one harassing Caroline, I'll be back. That's a promise."

"Is that a threat?" Marita called after his departing form.

"Take it for whatever you will."

Landon stalked from the apartment. When he reached the parking lot outside, he expelled a deep breath. He wasn't normally a vindictive man, but the outpouring of rage he now felt toward Marita left him feeling drained but determined.

Chapter Thirteen

The light on Caroline's office telephone buzzed red for what seemed like the thousandth time today. And she had only been at work four hours. *"Grrrrrr!"*

The only downside to Marita's sudden absence was having to play receptionist as well as general manager. Damn her for more reasons than one.

"Smooth and bright, Magic 97," she drawled into the handset and rolled her eyes. What could her dad have been thinking when he approved "Smooth and bright" as their signature liner? Sounded like an ad for a damn laxative.

"C—Caroline?" the voice on the other end of the line managed between muffled sobs.

"Sandy, is that you?"

"I'm afraid so," she answered, sniffling and blowing her nose loudly into the telephone. "I am also afraid that you aren't going to feel very 'smooth and bright' when I tell you my news."

What now? Caroline snapped the pencil she'd been holding in half. Tossing the pieces aside, she asked, "What's wrong?"

"First, let me assure you I'm okay. You don't have to worry about that."

"I am so glad."

"Caroline, remember that row of attractive mailboxes down on Vermilion Street—the ones with all the English ivy and great lattice work surrounding them—?"

"Ah-huh."

"Well—let me tell you, the Jag took them out like a combine in a cornfield."

Caroline choked. "The Jag did what?"

"Oh, b—but it's gonna be okay. The mechanic driving the tow truck assured me—"

"Tow truck? What tow truck?"

"Mr. Cribb's tow truck. You know he's a mechanic. Well, anyway, he says your Jaguar is gonna be just fine. That insurance should pay for most of the damage."

"Damage?"

"You'll be relieved to know, the suspension was quite smooth as your car bounced over those mailboxes. I hardly felt a thing. I guess you do get what you pay for. I would've never thought—"

"Bounced?"

"But only after the brakes failed. Now before you get too excited, the good news is Mr. Cribbs took me to Rent-A-Wreck and I've got us a nice Day-Glo orange Pinto to drive until the Jag is fixed."

Caroline sighed. "And I suppose it has a 'rent me' sign where the tag should be."

"How did you know?"

"Just a lucky guess, I suppose."

"What time should I pick you up?"

"Tell you what, Sandy. Go on home. I'll catch a ride with Landon. If you're sure you're okay, I will just see you in the morning."

When Caroline hung up, she banged her forehead on the desktop. *I've found it. I am in hell.*

Was this day ever going to end?

She kicked her pumps off under her desk and wiggled her toes. She looked forward to nothing more than a hot bath and few peaceful hours with Landon before his air shift.

"Hello, beautiful," Landon said, sticking his head inside the door. "Ready to call it a day?" Smiling, he came the rest of the way inside, a bouquet of fragrant white gardenias in his hand.

She pushed her chair from the desk and stood. "If you only knew, Landon." She took her purse from the bottom desk drawer. "I'll tell you all about it on the way home."

He blocked the exit. "Not so fast, aren't we forgetting something?"

She took the flowers, pressing them to her nose. The soft, sweetness of the petals was somehow comforting. "How did I ever make it without you, Landon Shafer? Thank you."

Tiptoeing to brush his lips with her own, she gave him a small kiss. Did she see an unspoken promise in his dark eyes? A pledge of forever, of family, of love. *Sure you did, Caroline.*

On the way home they passed Mr. Cribb's garage where the Jaguar stood sentinel, front end squashed like a bug.

"What the hell happened?" Landon asked.

"Sandy said the brakes failed going around the curve on Vermilion Street, took out a whole row of mailboxes."

Landon raked a hand through his hair. "I don't like this at all."

"Hell's bells. I don't like it either, but it was an accident."

⋯⊰❖⊱⋯

Sheldon Hunt's beach house had never seemed more welcoming. Caroline breathed a sigh as Landon pulled into the drive. She could see a small package propped between the screen and entry doors.

Clutching Landon's bouquet in one hand, she fumbled to retrieve the keys from her purse as she reached for the parcel with the other. "Thanks a lot for the hand. You are such a gentleman."

"If you wanted some help, all you had to do was ask," he replied, and took his hands out of the deep pockets of his jeans to assist.

Inside, Caroline dropped everything on the kitchen counter and rushed to the fridge to pour sweet tea.

"Want something to drink? I'm parched."

"Sure. Iced tea is fine."

"Fine, fine, fine," Caroline said, "Tea is fine. I'm fine. You're fine, everything is just blasted *fine!*" She lowered the tea pitcher to the countertop with force.

Landon ignored her outburst and continued to scrutinize the package. "There's no address on this."

"What do you mean? Of course there is. Otherwise, how was it delivered?" She set his glass on the counter and took a long drink from her own.

Landon gestured at the package. "Look, Caroline. I am telling you there is no address." He turned the box from side to side. "Nothing but plain brown paper."

A chill tiptoed up her spine. "Open it."

Instead, he gave the box a sound shake.

"Please be careful." She worried that it could be another snake, or worse. *Oh, my.* She hadn't told him about that— Fear suddenly rose like bile in her throat, tightening, choking off the words.

Landon pulled away the wrapping, which revealed nothing more than an ordinary shoe box. Cocking an eyebrow, he looked to Caroline. At her nod, he pulled out his Swiss Army knife and slit the tape. The kitchen clock ticked off the seconds, in rhythm with the heartbeat pulsing in her ears.

Landon swallowed and lifted the lid. The contents were hidden by neatly folded tissue paper. Slowly he folded the tissue paper back as if he were opening a Christmas gift.

A primal scream shattered the silence, just before the black hole surrounded her.

⊸⊰⟡⊱⊶

"Caroline, Caroline," the strain in Landon's voice brought her back to reality. His hands moved across her forehead, smoothing the wild tangle of her hair. He sat on the floor beside her.

"Come on, baby, wake up!"

She thought briefly of playing possum, just so he would continue to speak, every word affirming his affection. Instead she moaned and slowly opened her eyes.

"Sorry," she muttered, "I've never fainted before in my life."

"Under the circumstances I think you were entitled to a little faint. A Barbie doll with a razor embedded in her neck is a fairly twisted gift."

Caroline shuddered.

"You have to go to the police." His statement left no room for negotiation.

He reached down and pulled her into his arms. The strength of his body supported her. The mingled aromas of masculinity, a scent uniquely his, wafted to her. Comfort. In his dark gaze, she saw a reflection of herself. Of all the dreams she'd ever had or ever would.

"Let's go," he ordered. "Before I have to ravage you right here."

"That stings. Is sex all you want me for?"

"So shoot me, I see a beautiful woman unconscious on the floor, my mind wanders." He grinned.

Caroline mentally planned to blast him, but the phone rang diverting her attention. "Excuse me." She stood, went across the room and picked up the receiver.

"Yes?"

Dead silence.

"Who is this?"

Seeing she was visibly shaken, Landon grabbed the receiver from her hand and slammed it back into the cradle.

"Get your purse. We are going to the police station—now," he snapped, the good-natured teasing quickly replaced with urgency.

With Landon at her heels, Caroline grabbed her purse on the way out and headed for the Cherokee. Just as she cleared the doorway the insistent telephone screamed for attention. Again.

At her look, Landon motioned her to continue and he turned sharply on his heel to answer it.

Moments later he was snatching open the four-wheel-drive's door. He climbed in the driver's seat and tossed a paper sack summarily into the backseat.

"Is that what I think it is?" Caroline wrinkled her nose in distaste.

"Yep. There wouldn't be any point in going to the authorities without the evidence. We have no choice but to take the doll with us." He shrugged an apology.

As he started the Jeep and pulled out of the drive, Caroline shifted in her seat to pull the seat belt over her shoulder and snapped it into place. "Who was on the phone?"

He looked both ways, pulled onto Lake Shore Drive, and punched the accelerator. "We'll talk about it downtown."

So much for a quiet evening at home.

Beyond tired, Caroline smoothed a nonexistent wrinkle on the front of her skirt, twisted her hair round and round her index finger, then began to bite a fingernail. She knew what she was doing, but seemed powerless to stop the nervous actions.

Landon glanced over at her. "For goodness' sake. Would you be still?"

"Well, excuse me."

Focusing her gaze out the window, she tried to concentrate on the rapidly passing scenery. This only seemed to aggravate an already rising headache, so she closed her eyes and pressed her forehead against the cool glass.

It really was a terrifying notion. Someone watching her, waiting to attack. And she could do nothing to stop it. A mysterious stalker. Someone right in her midst.

Everyone had heard stories about celebrities being terrorized by obsessed fans, but the article she'd seen in this morning's paper had said that two thirds of all stalking victims were people who are not in the public eye.

Still, her situation seemed almost surreal. Miller Beach was a small township, the kind of place where families felt safe, felt sheltered from the crime that made headlines in larger cities.

Caroline tried to sort things out in her mind. It had all started with the faxes sent to her office. Faxes about extremely violent crimes against women. What happened next though, was what made her begin to think she was the victim of a stalker.

The harassment had increased in both frequency and intensity. The stakes elevated with each succeeding incident. Phantom phone calls, then the snake she now believed hadn't crawled in the open window. Surely the coral snake had been placed there by some unknown entity who meant to do her a great deal of bodily harm. And last but not least, the Barbie.

Could it have been meant to represent a voodoo doll of sorts?

Did some monster really mean to slit her throat?

Caroline shivered, the concept simply too much to bear.

Too, the list of suspects was short. Landon leaned toward Marita, with her strange phone calls to "Sinful Secrets" using "Kitten" as an alias. Not to mention her obvious personal interest in Landon. And the name change supposedly brought about by some kind of startling physical transformation. A change which Sandy had discovered quite by accident.

Wayne Nelson was also under consideration. But why? Why? Why? Vindictive enough? Yes. Cold and heartless enough? Without a doubt. Psychotic enough? Caroline had her doubts.

Perched on the edge of an old, extremely uncomfortable green Naugahyde chair Caroline eyed Chief Inspector King across the desk.

Landon stood gesturing emphatically as he spoke, explaining the events of the last few weeks, up to the arrival of the mutilated doll. "On the way out of the house to come here, I intercepted a call meant for Caroline."

He wiped his palms down the front of his jeans and glanced at her sharply. "Mr. Cribb, over at Miller Beach Mechanics, says the brakes on Caroline's Jaguar didn't simply fail."

"What did he say?" Caroline demanded as she rose from

her seat to face him.

He moved to place his hands on her shoulders, but he spoke to the chief. "The lines were cut. He believes someone intentionally sabotaged the Jag's braking system."

At that moment Caroline felt her diaphragm contract forcing the air from her lungs. "Oh my." Darkness threatened again, and she shook her head to keep it at bay. Then from some place deeper, a new sensation, more powerful than fear, surfaced. A surge of pure, unadulterated rage swept through her. With it, an incredible energy.

"I refuse to be a victim," she shouted. "Do you hear me?" She turned to the chief, who stood behind his desk. "I said, do you hear me?" She leaned over the desktop and poked him in the chest with her index finger. "I will do whatever it takes to protect myself from this lunatic. If that means carrying a gun everywhere I go, or shooting someone dead—then so be it! Life is too damn short to live in fear."

With that, Caroline turned on her heel and left, slamming the door behind her so hard that the sound seemed to echo through the entire building.

—⋇❖⋇—

"Well." The chief crossed his arms over the spot on his chest Caroline had targeted with her index finger. "I must say that is one helluva woman, young man."

Landon grinned. "I'm afraid you don't know the half of it, sir."

"Unfortunately, the little gal is right about one thing. She is going to have to pretty much look out for herself. At least until we have some evidence linking someone to these crimes. As it is, the most I can offer to do is to question the people you've mentioned. Frankly, Mr. Shafer, I wouldn't hold out much hope that either Ms. Taubold or Wayne Nelson will confess once we haul them down here."

"I appreciate anything you can do."

The chief nodded his understanding. "If you want my

advice, I wouldn't let the little lady out of my sight until this is over."

Landon shook hands with King, thanked him, and walked out the door.

—⋇⟨⟩⋇—

Two hours later, an officer knocked on Chief Inspector King's door; he gestured for him to bring the woman inside.

"Please have a seat, Ms. Taubold." King pointed to the green Naugahyde chair last occupied by Caroline Hunt. "Would you care for a cup of coffee? A cold drink?"

"No." Marita glared as she took a seat. "Being brought downtown to a police station does not make me thirsty. It makes me mad as hell."

The chief shifted his considerable weight from one foot to the other. "Oh, ho-ho. We have a little attitude, do we, Miss Taubold?" He narrowed his eyes, and absently rubbed the permanent five o'clock stubble on his chin.

The suspect planted fists on her slim hips. "The very least you could do would be to explain exactly what is going on. What am I being charged with?"

The inspector slipped his hands in his suit pockets. "Now, now, Ms. Taubold. You aren't being charged with anything. I just thought we could have a little chat. I need to ask you a few questions."

She raised a perfectly arched brow and straightened her back. "Such as?"

The chief took a seat and pulled a stack of papers in front of him. "Do you have any knowledge of threatening faxes sent to one Ms. Caroline Hunt?" He put on his best "to protect and serve" smile.

"No!"

"Have you been personally involved with or, know anyone involved in, harassing Ms. Caroline Hunt, in any way, shape, or form?"

"Of all the—" Marita rose indignantly from the chair.

"Did she tell you that? Oooh! What nerve. She is just jealous because Landon and I are...uh, somewhat involved." A sly smile. "That witch would do anything to come between us."

The chief cleared his throat and leaned back in his chair. "Funny you should mention Mr. Shafer. He just happened to be here with Ms. Hunt not very long ago. He told me of his suspicions where you are concerned, Kitten."

If looks could kill, Chief Inspector King knew he would have been sliced in two. Marita's eyes flashed red. She curled her manicured fingernails.

"Let me leave you with this, Chief," she hissed between her teeth. "If you've got a case, make it. If not, leave me the hell alone, or this department will be slapped with the mother of all harassment suits. Do I make myself perfectly clear?"

Finished, she smiled sweetly, pushed herself out of the chair with force, leaving a small smear on the chrome armrest.

Good girl, Kitten. You squeezed your hand 'til you bled. You've left me a gift, without even knowing it. Yes. There was just enough fresh blood on that chair arm to get a DNA sample.

He punched a button on his intercom. "Thelma, send up someone from forensics, ASAP. And be sure to tell them to bring an evidence kit."

Chief Inspector King laced his fingers behind his head and arched his back in a satisfied stretch.

—◆—

"Caroline Hunt's residence. Landon Shafer speaking."

"Shafer? This is Chief Inspector King."

At that moment, Landon was very glad Caroline had gone to lie down and that he was alone in the kitchen. "I'm surprised to hear from you so quickly, Chief. What can I do for you?"

"Thought you and your lady friend should know. Marita Taubold just left my office."

Hope against all hope! "Did she tell you anything useful?"

"Let me say this off the record." The chief's voice seemed to hold a conspiratorial tone. "If you repeat what I'm about to tell you to anyone, I'll deny I ever said it."

"I won't say anything. You have my word."

"Between me and you, Shafer, my gut tells me that lady is guilty as hell. For now, though, there's not one thing I can do about it. Just be careful.

"Thanks, Chief. I'll keep that in mind."

Actually, Landon had been working on a plan since the moment Chief Inspector King essentially told him not to let Caroline out of his sight. Now he knew exactly what he had to do. He picked up the handset once more, but this time he punched in Mike's home number.

Three rings, then, "Yo!"

"Hey, buddy. Just the man I need to talk to."

Chapter Fourteen

"What's up, man?"

Landon quickly gave Mike the lowdown on everything, as much as he could, ending with, "I think the best thing for us to do is to tell the listeners I'll be out of town for a couple of days. You can then run two previously taped 'Sinful Secrets' and bill it as 'The Best of Sinful Secrets.' No one but you, Caroline, and I will know I'm still around, that I am in fact watching the Hunt house. If we're lucky, Marita or Mary Jo or whatever the devil her name is, will make a move on one of those nights."

"Sounds like as good an idea as any," Mike said. "When do you want to do this?"

Landon sighed and massaged his temple. "I'll need to be back on the air, live, Valentine's Day, which is this Saturday, so let's go ahead and do it this Wednesday and Thursday."

"It's you're call."

"Thanks, Mike. See ya tonight."

Upstairs in her bedroom Caroline tossed and turned, unable to sleep. Memories played like a filmstrip in her mind. And it was so very real.

Too real—

Although Caroline was but seven years old when her mother died, she would never forget that night.

Dinah Hunt had been sick for days with what she'd called

a common cold. *Forever frugal, she had refused to see a doctor for such a small thing. "It's a waste of money," she'd claimed to both her husband and their housekeeper. "I'll be just fine."*

But she wasn't just fine.

It had all happened so quickly. Caroline shuddered at the remembrance and a chill crept up her spine—

Not yet six o'clock in the cool, dry evening that had been glazed by a setting autumn sun, she had made her frantic call to her father at the radio station.

"It's Mama. She's real sick." Her voice trembled. *"Daddy, her temperature is a hundred and three."*

"Try to calm down, baby," Sheldon said. *"I'll be right home."*

Over Dinah's protests, the housekeeper called in a doctor, the Hunt family's friend and neighbor, Layton Johns. He arrived quickly.

A matter of minutes later, at the first sound of her father's footfalls on the walkway, Caroline pulled the front door open. Running to meet him, clutching her much-beloved old pillow by a corner, she yanked at her father's coat sleeve all the way into the house.

She calmed somewhat when he cupped her face, his thumbs stroking her cheekbones in an attempt to console her. Then he bent and lifted his frightened little girl into the safety of his arms, cradling her there for a moment before he quickly made his way upstairs.

Sheldon came to a sudden halt just outside the bedroom he shared with his wife. The housekeeper stood next to the window twisting her apron in her hands. Dr. Johns sat studying Dinah Hunt above his half-glasses, a stethoscope pressed to her chest. Caroline couldn't see her mother, but she heard ragged, frenzied coughing and pitiful attempts at gasping for air.

"I don't understand," Sheldon said, his voice heavy with fear. *"What happened?"*

The housekeeper came forward. "We should take Caroline

downstairs and let the doctor finish examining Mrs. Hunt."

"Yes. Yes, of course."

Leading the way into the kitchen, Caroline's father shook his head and clutched his daughter even tighter in his arms. "I thought she was getting better," he said, as if to himself.

Caroline's shoulders hunched with sadness, the housekeeper set out milk and cookies that went untouched.

They all waited for word from Layton Johns. Time ticked in long, long seconds. Then Sheldon abruptly pushed himself from the counter he leaned against. Clasping his hands behind his back, he began pacing in a straight line up and down the room.

"What's taking so long? It seems like Layton's been in there forever."

In her most reassuring voice, the housekeeper said, "It hasn't been more than fifteen minutes."

"Is Mama going to the hospital?" Caroline asked.

Obviously forcing calm, Sheldon stroked his daughter's cheek. "That's just something we'll have to wait and see."

He straightened and shoved his hands in his pant pockets, turning to pace again. The moment Dr. Johns appeared in the kitchen doorway, three anxious, worried faces turned his way.

"How is she?" Sheldon moved toward him.

Layton Johns, surgeon, had deep sadness in his kind eyes as he sighed. He set his worn black medical bag on the floor, saying, "Dinah is very ill. You realize this is not my field...but I can tell you what she has is most certainly not a cold. It's pneumonia. And from the sound of it there may be an abscess in the left lung. I don't think the right one is much better—I can't be certain without seeing an x-ray. May I use your phone?"

"Are you going to call an ambulance?" Sheldon asked, going pale.

The doctor removed his glasses. For a moment, his face took on a haunted expression before he pressed a thumb and forefinger to the bridge of his nose. His gaze met Sheldon's as he replaced his glasses. "I'm going to tell you straight. As I

141

said before, this is not my field but—I seriously doubt Dinah can survive a trip to the hospital. I'm going to call Buford Thomas and ask him to come to the house. He's an internist, the best. Then I'll order oxygen from the hospital. Meanwhile, bathe her with cool cloths. We have to lower the fever."

Tears glistened in Sheldon's eyes, but he blinked them back and cleared his throat.

Caroline couldn't contain her tears as her father did; they brimmed and trickled down her cheeks. *Mama wants me to be brave.* She swallowed hard, straightening her small frame to its full height. "Mama's going to be all right," she announced.

Caroline's father placed his hand on her shoulder and squeezed, comforting as best he could.

The doctor crouched down and took both her smaller hands in his larger ones. "Your mother is very ill. There are some things we just can't—" He looked up at Sheldon. When he lowered his gaze, he continued. "I can't promise what Dr. Thomas and I do will be enough. Do you understand?"

Caroline nodded in slow motion, focusing on the floor, where she'd dropped her favorite old pillow, she couldn't recall when.

"Just remember—" Again Sheldon lifted her into his arms, bringing her close to his chest. "Your mother is very weak. She may not be able to fight the infection."

Caroline searched for some small bit of reassurance in first her father's eyes, then the doctor's. There was none.

Dr. Johns slowly lifted his medical bag from the floor. "All we can do is hope for a miracle. They do happen." Every word seemed to come from his heart. He centered on her father. "I'll make those calls now."

Less than an hour later, Dr. Thomas pronounced, "She's gone."

Sheldon's sobs broke the silence. Caroline threw herself at him, but he couldn't comfort her. Her father had always been strong, had never cried, had always known what to say at the right moment. But not then. The strong, fearless man Caroline had always known before this awful night had become a shad-

ow of his former self.

That had been so many years ago.

Dinah Hunt now lay buried in a beautiful cemetery at the north end of the island, in the first of the four plots her widower had purchased. He rested there, too. Caroline's parents were again together. The thought comforted her. Except that two plots waited—

No!

It was then that she caught sight of Landon standing beside her bed, the soft light from the hallway behind him. He said nothing as he took her into his arms and to give comfort. His chest was as solid as a wall. All of him was. He was the only man other than her father who'd ever made her feel safe.

My father let me down when Mama died.

Would Landon let her down, too? But had her father known something about his former stepson that his daughter couldn't understand? What was the full intent behind that last will and testament? Apparently Sheldon Hunt had wanted his daughter to be with Landon—

"Caroline?" Landon's hand touched her shoulder. "Shhh, baby. I'm here. Why are you crying? Tell me what's wrong."

She turned toward him, needing his warmth to chase away the chill of her thoughts.

"What is it?" he asked, stroking her hair.

"I—I don't want to talk about it," she whispered. "Just hold me, Landon."

He did, and blessedly asked no more questions.

Caroline could not bring herself to discuss her memories. She wanted only to hold him tightly.

"You're not alone now. I'm here."

But for how long?

She put her arms around his neck. After a few moments, her gaze searched Landon's face. She slid her fingers into his dark hair. The sleek texture and his closeness made her shiver with pleasure and say his name as she watched him with wide, wondering eyes.

"Are you all right?" he asked. "You're looking at me as

though you've never seen me before."

"I haven't. Not in the way I do now. Kiss me, Landon. Kiss me hard."

The kiss he gave her was deep and hot and hungry. When it ended, he said, "I want you to listen, because I'm going to say this only once. Do you understand?"

She slowly nodded her head.

Apparently satisfied, he continued. "I have already had all the shallow relationships and quick women I've ever wanted in my life. I want more than that out of life."

He moved his entire body more fully to hers, where she felt the rise and fall of his breathing beneath the wide expanse of his chest.

"I, too, want more than a meaningless relationship," she admitted.

"What is it that you want?" He lessened what little space there was between them.

They were so close that she reveled in the hard press of his body against hers. She lost herself in those deep brown eyes; her pulse quickened at what would come. She wanted this man with all her heart and soul. He was all that mattered now. The regrets, if there were to be any, would be for later.

"I want you," she whispered as his mouth closed over hers and he flattened her against the mattress beneath them.

She accepted his compelling warmth. His hands gentle, they moved skillfully through her hair and down to hold her face. His warm and soft lips kissed her deeply. A yearning ache encompassed her; her breasts tingled with a sweet aching fire. It consumed her.

The insatiable need of him caused a guttural sound to escape her throat of its own accord, from some great depth in her. The sound caused his body to respond in kind.

His hands moved to where her breasts rounded and she moaned. Their hearts hammering in rhythm, he raised his lips from hers and buried his face in her hair.

Caroline ran her hand softly along the side of his chiseled face. He groaned and caught her wrist in one hand and with agonizing slowness, he lowered his lips and kissed it.

An instant later he drew her to her knees. "Do you want me, Caroline?"

"Oh, yes—"

"Say it then. Say you want me. I need to hear you say the words."

"I—I want you. I need you."

"You're sure?"

She threw her arms around his neck as she softly, slowly ran her tongue up and down the length of his neck.

He shivered.

"Does that answer your question?" she asked in a throaty whisper.

He pulled back, assessing her, a smile curving his full lips, and nodded his head in wonder as he cupped his large hands boldly under her bottom. "Oh, yes. It does answer my question. Quite well, in fact," he said fiercely. Then his fingers were enmeshed in her waves.

"I want you, too," he said in a throaty rasp of a whisper and he kissed her thoroughly before gently lowering her to the mattress again. Still he kissed her, and her soft moans pressed against his mouth.

It was as if she slept and this was a wonderful dream. As if none of this were at all real. All too soon, the kiss ended. He dispensed with her sweater, undid the tiny hooks at the back of her bra and slowly removed the undergarment from her flesh to toss it aside, baring her breasts to him.

He drew back, his gaze resting on her raised nipples. He groaned before he paid an all too brief homage to each of them with the callused tips of his fingers, then each in turn, with the tip of his tongue.

Her head fell back and she gasped with a pleasure denied her for far too long. She took a deep breath, closed her eyes and thought, *This can't be.* Just when she had almost convinced herself she was having a delicious dream, he chuckled hoarsely and brought her back to reality. She was more than a little unsure about what she knew they were about to do.

As if Landon sensed the mental battle that raged within her, he placed his hand beneath her head and brought her close against him. "I told Sandy to go home right after I sent you upstairs to take a nap."

"Really?"

"Really," he said with a devilish smile.

She allowed her forehead to rest against his solid, comforting chest. His arms encircled her waist with a power both comforting and protective. She felt truly safe for the first time in days—no, years—and the warm stirrings for him increased. All her doubts and fears seemed to melt away with his tender, demanding touch.

He gave her a reassuring squeeze and continued to hold her steadfast. "I'm not, Wayne. I am not even the man I used to be," he whispered into her hair, understanding evident in every word he uttered.

She responded to his gentle caring, his substance. She raised happy eyes to his and smiled. "I know," she said simply. "I know."

Placing tentative hands on his shoulders, she lifted her lips to his and softly, sensuously kissed him. While continuing the kiss, deepening it with each passing moment, she slid her palms down to his shirtfront and began to slowly undo one button at a time. Leaving his mouth, she laid soft, moist lips on the newly bared skin of his chest each time she moved to undo the next button.

By the time she finished her intended task, Landon was gasping for air as if he might surely die of the agonizing pleasure. He said he craved her as if he were a man who was lost in the desert, craving water. Never in his life had he felt such a primitive need of anything.

At her urging, he slowly removed the rest of her clothing and poised himself above her. He moaned loudly and closed his eyes as her hand moved down to release the button and zipper of his pants and removed them along with his underwear. He gasped as his body stiffened above her when she stroked him tenderly with her fingers. His head thrust back and his voice became full with sweet words. She caught him firmly in both hands and molded him into magnificence; his body trembled and sweat beaded across the broad expanse of his chest. He submitted to her ministrations, but only for so long, only until he murmured that he could not hold back much longer.

He gently but firmly removed her hands from him and after parting her legs, began dispensing similarly agonizing pleasures on her, with his hands. He stroked her thighs, kneading her buttocks, as he kissed his way up to her aching breasts. She withered under his touch, tossing her head shamelessly from side to side, uttering mindless words of passion.

She gasped with long-denied pleasure as he again encircled each pulsating nipple in turn with his tongue. Her nipples puckered into taut dusky, moist buds and her breasts ached for his suckle. Fiercely, her fingers entangled in his ebony waves and pulled him more fully to her. She begged but he still denied her only grazing them lightly with his teeth. She tossed her head from side to side and raised her hips to him, beckoning him.

Finally as if the torment had become too unbearable for him, he took full suckle, at first one breast and then the other. She cried out with the pleasure and her hands began to move frantically up and down his corded back as a warm moistness filled her.

"Take me," she demanded hoarsely. "Take me, now. I need you."

That was all it took to make him seek her moist warmth with an intensity he had never known. He gave a raw, almost primitive cry as he lifted her hips and entered her with one fierce welcomed thrust. Instinctively, her legs closed around his hips and brought him more deeply within her.

He seemed lost in a world where only they existed. He held his hands firmly beneath her bottom, delving deeper and deeper with each new thrust. She rose on the tide of passion first and weeping with a pleasure never known to her before, her body went into unrelenting waves of completion.

Seconds passed before she began to regain a semblance of

normal breathing. She opened her eyes to see his magnificent face contorted with passion. She was filled with awe as she realized the power she wielded over this wonderful creature.

Holding him closely, she caressed him and whispered her needs as she fell into the tender rhythm he set. Now it was he who taunted shamelessly. He mouthed unintelligible words of passion as his body stiffened, again and again, then finally released.

Sated, he fell to her and she welcomed the massive weight of his body on hers. They lay that way for a long time, bodies intertwined, the two of them now one.

Chapter Fifteen

The next morning Caroline stared at the clutter on her desk. Mountains of spreadsheets, profit-and-loss statements, and market research. All of which must be studied. Relevant information committed to memory, and then the entire mess filed neatly away for future reference.

She stretched, rubbed her eyes, and swiveled around in her chair. Her business tasks seemed overwhelming. How her father had managed to make it look so easy was beyond her.

Sheldon Hunt would have said, "It looks easy because I have you to help me, honey." The thought warmed her, and to some extent, it was true. But her father had been the sun, she and the staff merely the planets, each in orbit around him. He'd given them the energy, drive, and desire to succeed. Caroline was sure he would be disappointed in her now. Hell, she was disappointed in herself!

He'd always told new account executives, "Sales are effortless."

To prove his point he had also maintained the top sales position during his entire tenure at the station. When sales-people complained that he had all the choice clients, he would cull his list, assigning his most lucrative accounts to them. Then starting from scratch, he would hit the street, cold-calling on every business in the listening area that wasn't already advertising. He always delivered. And he always delivered what he promised for the businesses that trusted him with their advertising dollars. His absence was keenly felt at Magic 97 and in the entire business community.

Caroline blinked back tears. She could almost hear the

sound of his voice, echoing down the hall during one of his infamous Prayer Meetings, as he had always referred to the weekly staff conferences that kept everyone on their toes.

Sheldon's motto had been, "Never ask anyone to do a job that you can't or won't do yourself." She had received no preferential treatment either. No nepotism. She had been required to start at the bottom and work her way up, just as everyone else had. Consequently, there wasn't one piece of equipment in the building she couldn't operate or repair. And she had, on more than one occasion, been required to pinch hit an air shift, which admittedly wasn't her forte. But better than dead air, no doubt.

She thought, *I am my father's daughter, sales and public relations my first love. Yet, since his death I've failed to conduct one sales meeting or do anything to unify the staff.* It just seemed that the time hadn't been there. Or the desire. Caroline turned to gaze at Sheldon's portrait, painted several years before his death. Tears fell then, slipping soundlessly down her cheeks.

"Oh, Daddy! What am I going to do?"

His voice seemed to echo across the years, a conversation they had when she and Landon were teenagers.

Heavy-metal music was just coming into vogue, lyrics glamorizing drug use, violence, the degradation of women. Landon, always a cutting-edge kind of guy, could not understand why in light of the music's popularity, Sheldon refused to play it.

His answer to the question was the benchmark of their organization. "We do not own Magic 97. The people of Miller Beach do. The public trust is an awesome responsibility. This is a small market. I have to look my listeners in the eye every day. If my decisions aren't hip or trendy, or even if they cost us money, so be it. My personal integrity is wrapped up in the reputation of this facility. I would close up shop before I'd allow that to be tarnished."

Sheldon Hunt would roll over in his grave if he knew "Sinful Secrets" now owned the overnights!

150

In light of all that had happened since the show's debut, surely even Landon would have to concede that "shock" radio just did not belong on Magic 97.

Caroline rose and walked to the window. How she wished she was Atlas so that she could shrug what she felt was the weight of the world off her shoulders.

With an expansive breath, she rested folded arms on the high sill and gazed out the window. A group of smiling children jumped rope on the playground across the street. Buttery sunlight peeked through the branches of the ancient oaks, casting broken shadows on their faces. Had she ever been that young, that carefree? A motherless child early on, how she had longed for a mommy to brush her hair, to read her stories, or to sing to her.

Sheldon had done his best, but Caroline had to ask herself if her choices in life had somehow been tied to the lack of a significant female role model. Was her desire for a child of her own an attempt to fill the void left when her mother died? Was it too much to want a family and a career? Wayne Nelson had certainly thought so.

It was at that moment when Caroline realized her husband had been abusive. She never really knew the comforts of a healthy marriage. It didn't occur to her that it was uncommon to walk on eggshells to keep the peace. To be asked to sacrifice dreams to satisfy a spouse. For Wayne to blame her career for the miscarriage was completely unfair. Yes. That had definitely been abusive behavior. Perhaps Wayne's want of a divorce had been a blessing in disguise. Perhaps? No. It was.

As a child, all she had really wanted was a real family. A mom and dad, brothers and sisters. When Sheldon had married Landon's mother, Caroline briefly believed her dream had come true, only to find Lee remote and unapproachable, sinking deeper and deeper into the pit of alcoholism. After the divorce, Lee's suicide had cost them all so much. Sheldon's unwarranted guilt, her bitter disappointment—and Landon's rage. He was raging still.

Caroline reached for a tissue, blew her nose, and resumed

her position at the window. It seemed that Landon would spend his life pushing the edge of the envelope. In some ways, she wished she were more like him. The creative, free spirit.

Someone had to be responsible. She had always been and would always be that person. She was certain that was why her father had left her in charge of the station, a heavy burden to bear at times. Frankly, Caroline resented the leeway Sheldon Hunt had afforded his stepson during their youth. She supposed her father felt sorry for him, losing his mother the way he had.

In Miller Beach, when Landon would get out of hand, the local police would simply drop him off at home. But when he went to the University of Georgia, that was another story entirely. There the cops locked him up.

Caroline shook her head. She could not remember how many times Sheldon had to driven up to Athens in the middle of the night to bail Landon out. It took him five years to finish a four-year degree. Not because he wasn't smart, but because he didn't care. Too, he had little time to study, what with the distraction of wine, women, and song. Like General Sherman, Landon burned Atlanta, and cut a path to the sea. Would he ever be someone she could trust, depend on, in business or in life?

Sure, he'd claimed to want a stable relationship, but claiming and making one out of what they had were two different things.

She bit her thumbnail nervously. While their intimate time together had been wonderful, she had to remind herself he hadn't made any promises. He might not even want to settle down and grow up. She would just have to keep her eyes open and heart closed. If not, she might just get it broken again.

The light on the playground began to dim, drawing her attention. The children started leaving with their parents. With a deep sigh, Caroline straightened her shoulders. Enough of this introspection! She had work to do.

One day ran into the next. Caroline plowed methodically through the papers on her desk. "What I wouldn't do for a good temp!"

A sales contract caught her eye. "Oh, the logs," she groaned. No logs, no commercials, no advertising dollars! Moreover, she'd have to do traffic herself.

Caroline rushed through the building to the reception area, which had formerly been Marita's domain. The logs represented the station's inventory of thirty- and sixty-second commercials. Day, part, and length of the spot determined rates.

If the logs were messed up, Caroline wouldn't know what had run at what time, or for which business. She would have no way to figure her billing.

"If Marita has screwed this up, I'll track her down and kill her myself." Caroline tapped on the keyboard and waited for the computer to boot up.

When it did, she opened the traffic program, which contained Magic 97's billing records and logs. She gaped in horror. All the records had been deleted.

"Why, you little—"

It could be fixed, but doing so would take hours if not days to repair. The computer generated daily, weekly, and monthly statements. Furthermore, the reports were done at the beginning of the month, so most of it would not yet be on printout. "Oh!"

She would just have to piece everything together as best she could, with the written order forms from the sales department. Copies of these for the week-to-date should be in Marita's bottom desk drawer.

This, of course, was locked.

"It's a good thing you have already left, Marita Mary Jo. If you were still here, I would fire your ass on the spot," Caroline muttered, as she worked the lock with a paper clip. Finally, it opened.

Her eyes flew wide with indignation. "You bastard," she hissed.

Caroline lifted the shirt she knew was Landon's from the drawer. She had only seen him wear this particular garment about a hundred times! The cloying scent of Marita's cheap perfume permeated the material.

"Oh, Landon—" She blinked back tears of disappointment.

Chapter Sixteen

Several hours later Caroline squinted, the characters on her computer screen a fuzzy blur. *I really need a break!*

The most pressing problem, scheduling commercial breaks for the next few days, was accomplished. The rest would have to wait until she had gotten some rest and her head quit pounding.

She walked to the office sofa and fingered Landon's soiled shirt. Her gut clenched in response. She could think of only one reason Marita would have an article of his clothing in her desk. It broke her heart to think Landon could have been sleeping with both of them. Although with his record of sexual accomplishments, Caroline did not know why she was shocked. As she'd always said, a square will always have four sides, and Landon would never change.

She moved across the room to the window. Dusk, her favorite time of day. Usually. Perhaps a walk in the brisk air would help clear her head. Thus, she grabbed a light jacket from the hall tree by the door, slipped it on, and headed outside.

Aimlessly, she wandered along the main street of town. She forced herself to think about scenery. It was beautiful even now. In February, when most of the country was frozen in the white grip of winter, the skies above Miller Beach wept misty tears at twilight. The first green buds on azalea bushes optimistically expected an early spring. The dull roar of the ocean several blocks away was as constant and familiar as her own breathing.

Entranced, Caroline stopped in the middle of the sidewalk and sightlessly gazed at the garish window display of Valentine's Day goods in Franklin's Five and Dime.

"You love Landon Shafer," she said to her reflection in the glass. The futility of that truth sent a tear slipping down her cheek.

Caroline walked half a block to Doy's Drugstore, with its soda fountain in the back. She virtually fell into the red vinyl booth as she called out, "A Cherry Coke, please, Mr. Binkley," to the owner behind the counter.

She stared down at her hands where they were locked together on the Formica tabletop. Doy Binkley sat the icy fountain drink on the table. "You all right?"

"Yeah, I'm okay," she said quietly.

Mr. Binkley shrugged and ambled back to the cash register. She'd heard that folks were saying she had changed since her father's death. That she wasn't herself. It just went to show that some gossip was true. The lady in this booth didn't act at all like the usual Caroline Hunt.

Sipping her drink, she wished she'd ordered a hot chocolate instead. Landon Shafer, how could you do it?

She should have known the truth when she asked him if he had slept with Marita and he had responded by saying that "sex and a love affair were not the same thing at all."

How could she have been so very wrong?

He was convincing as hell, that was how!

Her eyes narrowed as she stared down into her glass. He had kissed her, made love to her, as a man does to the woman he loves. Murmured all the right words in response to her own husky whispers. Lies, all lies.

She sighed. If he murmured nothing but lies, they were the sweetest lies she had ever heard. And she'd fallen hook, line, and sinker. Payback time is hell and this was hers, for moving Landon from "Morning Drive" to overnights.

"Aren't you going to drink up?" Sandy slid into the seat across from her, drawing her out of her dark study. "What's wrong? You're as pale as a ghost."

Caroline pulled the cola to her and took a sip through the straw. "The question is, Sandy, what is right?" Two tears escaped simultaneously and rolled down her cheeks. "The answer? Nothing."

Sandy made a *tsk-tsk* sound. "Surely things can't be all that bad."

"Would you care to bet?" Caroline replied softly, not wanting anyone to overhear. Her eyebrows knitting together.

Sandy patted her hand, a thoroughly feminine gesture of comfort. "Why don't you tell me about it, dear?"

Her sympathy served only to make Caroline cry that much harder. "It's just awful. Since Daddy died, everything's gone wrong." She hiccuped. "Losing him was bad enough. Now someone is stalking me. Before Marita quit, she was kind enough to screw up my billing records. And last, but not least, I find Landon's shirt in her desk drawer."

"Is that all you'rrewhining about? I thought you might have some real troubles," Sandy said with a good-natured grin.

Caroline shot her a dirty look.

Sandy held up both hands. "Just trying to lighten up the conversation."

"I'm furious with myself for hoping Landon and I might actually have something meaningful together." Caroline finished her Coke too quickly and blinked hard against the blinding pain of the icy headache, as Sandy gave her a sympathetic look.

"What makes you think Landon doesn't care for you?"

"Why would you think Marita hid his shirt in her desk? She's obviously worn it. That awful perfume she wears is all over it."

"Perhaps there's a logical explanation. You're always so quick to think the worst where Landon is concerned. Just maybe you should ask him about it and withhold judgment until he has an opportunity to explain himself. What a novel thought." Sandy graced her with a wink and a trace of a smile. "Imagine, Caroline Hunt allowing the man to speak his peace before she condemns him to death."

"My goodness, it's not as if this is Landon's first offense or anything, you know. He probably has the longest rap sheet of love in modern history."

Sandy cocked her head to one side. "In this great land, a man is presumed innocent until proven guilty. Regardless of his prior record."

"Well, thank you, Madam Justice, for your support."

"Just trying to be fair. You might want to give it a whirl yourself." Sandy glanced at her watch. "Gotta go. See ya in the A.M. That is, if I still have a job."

"Makes one wonder, doesn't it?" Caroline rose, dropping change on the table to cover the cost of her drink and a tip. "I'll walk out with you."

She linked arm with Sandy's, and they left the drugstore. Two blocks down the street, they parted.

"By the way." Caroline smiled at her friend. "You do still have a job."

―≈≫❖≪≈―

The phone was ringing off the hook when Caroline walked in the beach house. Before she could pick up, the machine clicked on and her recorded message greeted the caller.

"Caroline, if you're there, pick up, it's me."

She rolled her eyes. *Landon!* She was not in the mood.

"Caroline, I know you're there. If you don't pick up I'm coming over."

She ignored the evident worry in his tone and fixed herself a glass of iced tea. She then settled on the sofa with the Miller Beach Journal and tried to read. Three more times the phone rang and she allowed the machine to pick up.

Not fifteen minutes later he wasn't knocking at her door, he was kicking it down.

Caroline dropped the paper at the sound of the crash. "What the—?"

Landon surged through the door like Thor, the god of thunder, entering Valhalla. "Caroline!"

158

She jumped to her feet, knocking over her tea glass and ran straight to Landon, to punch him directly in the center of his chest.

Rubbing the abused area, he asked, "What the hell did you do that for?"

Fists planted on her hips, she replied, "Why the hell did you kick my door down?"

"I thought you were in trouble! You didn't pick up the phone. When I saw your car in the driveway, I figured you might need help."

"Well, I don't. Especially not from the likes of you, Landon Shafer."

"Let's back up and punt here. I'm lost. You're mad at me? Would you mind telling me, what for?"

"As if I didn't have enough problems—now I find out you're a two-timing, egg-sucking dog."

"I guess I'm a deer caught in the headlights here, 'cause I don't know what to say." He turned his hands, palms up. "Would you care to expound, since I fail to catch your drift so far?

"You're telling me that if I find a shirt of yours in Marita's desk drawer, I'm not supposed to believe you've been sleeping with her!"

"Are my eyes rolling? Because I don't know what the hell you're talking about."

Caroline walked back to the couch, snatched up the shirt in question and threw it at him.

He caught it, but hesitated and held up an index finger. "Then again—maybe I do."

A moment lapsed as she rallied composure. "So you admit you slept with her while you were sleeping with me?"

"Hell, no. I'm not admitting to that, or anything else at this point. Just shut up and sit down. We have something important to discuss."

Shut up? How dare he? But she kept her lips clamped. If she hadn't been in shock she wouldn't have obeyed. As it was, the fight went out of her. So she sat.

159

He followed suit and put Caroline's hand in his. "Listen. I don't know when she took the shirt, but I assume it was the night she stayed over."

Caroline tried to stand, but Landon hung on to her hand to keep her from leaving. "Nothing happened. I swear it." He gave the three-fingered salute, as if that lent more credibility to his statement.

"Why should I believe anything you have to say?" she wanted to know as he pulled her back down onto the sofa once more.

"Because it's the truth. Marita called me in the middle of the night not too long ago and said someone had broken into her house. I went over, she was upset, the police were there, and her window was in pieces. Trying to be a nice guy, I had her sleep over at my place. But she slept in my room and I slept on the sofa." He paused to take a breath. "She must have taken the shirt then, because that's the only time she has ever been to my place."

Caroline felt a little foolish. Sandy had been right. She always seemed to think the worse where Landon was concerned—

She reached up, touched his cheek, and grinned. "I believe you. But who's going to fix my front door?"

Before Landon left for the station later that night, he tucked Caroline snugly in bed. The short nap he'd managed hadn't been nearly enough, but it was better than nothing. He locked the front door behind him, which had been repaired at an exorbitant cost for emergency service, billed to his credit card.

The cool evening air revived him a bit. Boy, was he tired. He sure couldn't wait for this whole mess to be over. He couldn't remember the last time he'd had a full night's sleep.

He decided to drive by Marita's on the way to the station. Surprisingly, there were no lights on inside and no beige VW Bug in the parking lot. He wondered, if she did drive a Bug, where did she keep it?

Maybe it wasn't Marita following Caroline at all. Perhaps, someone else. Maybe Wayne Nelson was the one. Crazy, that Wayne had no reason to hurt Caroline, did he? What had she ever done to Wayne? She'd said Wayne had always been jealous of her friendship with him. How jealous?

And why would that make Wayne want to hurt her? Was Wayne hiding a hatred of Landon so deep that he would attack Caroline?

Apparently, she'd seen him only that one time in her office; she said he'd made no threat. Too, when Chief Inspector King had tried to bring him in for questioning, Wayne had already left town.

Landon raked his fingers through his hair. Too much had happened on too little sleep. His mind could not process it all. He would have to take a caffeine IV just to make it through tonight's broadcast.

"Hey, Mike," Landon called as he walked in the station. The program manager was pouring a cup of coffee. "Make that two, and make mine a double."

"Sure thing, boss. Fifteen minutes until Mustang Mike signs off."

He nodded. "Remember, tomorrow you're running 'The Best of Sinful Secrets.' I have one more favor to ask. All my listeners will know I'm out of town, so I can't drive the Cherokee. Everyone knows it's my vehicle. Can I trade cars with you for a couple of days?"

"Sure, I'll sacrifice for the cause and drive the Cherokee." Mike almost choked on his coffee. "You're more than welcome to my Tempo."

"You are so kind, pal." Landon scorched his tongue as he took a swig of coffee. "Ow!"

Mike glanced at his watch, "Whoops, five minutes 'til showtime. We better be hittin' and gettin'."

Landon pitched his coffee in the trash. Hope I can still talk with my tongue burned off.

—⊱⋆⊰—

As usual, Landon went on the air at precisely midnight.

"Magic 97—today's best music. I'm Landon Shafer, your host for 'Sinful Secrets,' a cutting edge show on after midnight hosted by adults—for adults—right here on the dial. Pick up the phone, 555-FANTASY, to call and share your most sinful secret or sexual fantasy. That number again, 555-FANTASY."

He turned off the microphone and looked at Mike behind the glass. "How many calls do we have waiting?"

"The board is full, man."

Landon fidgeted. He wondered if Marita would call in tonight as Kitten. Surely not, not after he'd confronted her. "Throw me one just a soon as this commercial is over."

The white clock on the wall with large black numbers ticked off two minutes. He began to sweat.

Finally, Mike tapped on the glass. "Hey, man. You aren't going to believe this but I've got Kitten on line three. You want me to just leave her hangin'?"

He released an expansive breath and put on his headphones. "No. I want to take it. But just pay attention this time, Mike. Okay?"

"I hear you. I hear you."

Thirty seconds later, the On-Air light illuminated above Landon's door and Mike held up a hand. He signed with his fingers—three, two, one—then pointed and mouthed, "You're on."

"Magic 97 and 'Sinful Secrets.' Your chance to share your utmost sexual fantasies every weeknight from midnight 'til two. We've got our first caller. Hi, you're on the air."

Dead air.

Not again, he bemoaned inwardly.

"Hi, you're on the air."

Still, no response. He glanced at Mike, who shrugged.

"Caller, are you there?"

"Oh, yes, Landon—I'm here—"

It was her. He was sure of it. "Would you care to give us your name?"

She ignored his question. "I hear you've been a very bad boy lately."

For some reason the female voice on the other end still did not sound like Marita's, even though he knew he couldn't be that wrong. But she could be doing any of a number of things to disguise her voice—

"I am always a bad boy," he quipped, trying to make light of the comment.

"My fantasy tonight is about you. Do you still want to hear it?" she challenged in a throaty whisper.

Now he was getting mad. "Sure. I'm game for anything. And I do mean anything." He paused to take a calming breath.

"Listeners, if you've just tuned in, we are on the air with a woman who says her fantasy tonight is about me. Me, of all people. Can you believe it? Caller, are you still on the line?"

"Oh, yes. Most definitely."

"All right, then. What is your fantasy?"

A loud crack reverberated over the telephone line.

"Oh, man. That sounded ominous. Care to tell us what that was?"

"That was my cat o' nine tails."

Landon swallowed. It had been the crack of a whip. The last thing he'd expected. He looked over at Mike, just to see if he was paying attention. And he was, thankfully. Landon exhaled, but before he could think of what to say—

She went on:

"Instantly I swing you around, pinning your hands behind your back in leather cuffs. I blindfold you. Then I unsnap your pants and pull the shoes off your feet. Totally strip you. I take you into a candlelit room, lift your hands over your head, hang your wrists up on a hook, above you. Only then do you begin to be sorry for being such a bad, bad boy—"

To Landon, it sounded more like something out of a book

rather than a real fantasy.

Again, the whip's crack.

Fed up with this little game of hers, he cleared his throat. "Sounds interesting, caller. But since you've already said this fantasy is about moi, I happen to know for a fact you have never acted this fantasy out with me before. So asking you my usual question would be a waste of time—"

"True," she said, cutting him off. "But I plan to. And very soon."

"Is that so—?"

"Oh, yes. It's so."

"You seem to forget, it takes two to tango."

"Oh, I'll remember. Don't you worry about that—"

Landon raised an eyebrow at Mike. That had sounded too ominous by half. "If, and I do mean if, you get the chance, which I can almost guarantee you won't—do you actually think you'd get what you wanted out of all this?"

"Oh, most definitely."

What would make you happy?" he asked.

"I told you before. I'm not the type of woman who takes no for an answer, remember? I'm going to get what I want."

The line went dead. Again.

At Landon's loss for words, Mike jumped in, "Well, stick a fork in it, listeners. She is done!"

Chapter Seventeen

The following evening Landon parked the borrowed Tempo half a block down from Caroline's house on Lake Shore Drive. He would like to have been closer. He would like to have been inside, in her bed, in her body.

He spoke aloud to himself in the darkness. "Whew, buddy, better not go there or it'll be one helluva long night." The depth and timbre of his voice startled even him, here within the confines of the compact car.

Landon raked his hair and blew the steam from the top of the Styrofoam coffee cup. He pulled small binoculars from the glove compartment, focusing on the mailbox by the street.

He panned the area. The repaired Jaguar stood vigil in the drive. He shook his head and smiled. He still couldn't believe Sandy had actually decided to buy the orange Pinto. *Oh well,* he thought. At least the man from Rent-A-Wreck was happy.

From this vantage point, Landon could see the front door unobstructed by a stand of oaks bordering the drive. The north facade and backyard were also clearly visible due to a slight bend in the road. He lowered the binoculars and sipped his coffee. The southern exposure would have to remain unguarded. There was simply no way for him to view all four sides of the house from this oceanside position.

An overgrown rosebush had all but taken over the south-facing retaining wall. Thick ropy runners and what he knew to be inch-long thorns, tough and sharp as tacks, should deter anyone attempting illegal entry from that end of the property.

Landon decided this would be as good a time as any to

inspect the weaponry he'd brought along. With considerable difficulty, due to the length of his legs and limited space, he pulled the small Beretta from the holster strapped to his calf. The gun was warm to his skin and seemed tiny, even toylike in his large hand. It was also fully loaded. He had seen to that at home.

He disarmed the safety and slipped the gun carefully back into the holster, saying a silent prayer that he wouldn't blow his foot off in the process.

On the passenger seat lay an awesome tool of destruction. A stainless-steel Glock 9mm shimmered and glowed in the moonlight. Landon carefully picked it up, hefting it in his right hand, attempting to become accustomed to the weight and feel of it. He studied the contours and lines, as one might a fine sculpture. After a time, he placed it back on the seat and wiped his sweaty palm on the thigh of his jeans.

The final concession to self-defense was an extremely sharp knife, cleverly disguised as a belt buckle. A gift from his friends, the Bowens of Lake Blackshear. They manufactured fine hunting knives. This little beauty was a specialty item, and Landon had thoroughly enjoyed it over the years. It had been honed from one piece of stainless steel. The blade could be concealed in a pouch on the backside of his belt. This little gem had gotten him out of more than one scrape in the "open-knife jukes" he tended to frequent in his younger days.

Turning the knife over in his hand, he contemplated the possibilities of actually cutting someone. He never had, had used it solely as a scare tactic. If he had his way, guns and knives would go unused and a peaceful solution found to the situation.

A coil of foreboding, dark as the night-shrouded Atlantic, suddenly tightened his gut.

Moonlight glinted off the blade like a mirror as he returned the knife to its proper place. He hunched deeper into his leather jacket. He was still cold, with the air in the car stale and stifling. He cranked down the window in spite of the low temperature. Somehow, he felt it would be preferable to freeze than to suffocate.

The street had fallen into near-black stillness. His eyes traced the path to Caroline's house, as one window, then another went dark, until the only light emanating from the house came from her bedroom. He imagined her preparing for bed. Pulling his tattered football jersey over her head, snuggling in the deep softness of the mattress. He hoped it would give her some comfort, the jersey as well as knowing he was outside watching the grounds.

Thoughts of Caroline brought feelings—unbidden, unwanted, unwelcomed. Landon squirmed, trying without much success to find a more comfortable position. Finally, he settled with his back against the driver's door, his right foot caught on the edge of the passenger's seat, his left foot sprawled on the floorboard below. He crossed his arms over his chest. Not much better, he decided, but at least his knees weren't wedged around his ears.

Landon knew he tried, like most men, to stay as busy as humanly possible to avoid situations where deep thought and introspection were the only available pastimes. Yet, dammit, here he was, the endless night stretching out before him like the mouth of a darkened tunnel.

And in that tunnel was a great wellspring of knowledge. Caroline was there, waiting to share all the mysteries of life. He was afraid. But the weight of the life he had lived pushed him toward her outstretched hand. Finally he closed his eyes and reached for her. When he opened them he stood toe to toe with his past.

Landon had to concede he measured his life in the days, months, and years since he first met Caroline. The culmination of experience that came before? It amounted to nothing in his estimation.

With the marriage of his mother and Sheldon Hunt had come the hope of a better life. Those dreams shattered quickly as Lee's drinking accelerated. Then after the divorce, she stayed drunk out of her mind, day and night. He could barely stomach being in the same room with her. He had avoided his mother.

When she'd died, he became overwhelmed with guilt. It was a very bad time; she'd been his salvation. She, too, had left him, using some misguided sense of family honor as an excuse.

On the day his mother died, he remembered next to nothing. In fact, there seemed to be great chunks of his childhood and adolescence missing. He had heard someone say that such repression came by the grace of God, a protection the mind offers the spirit when life is too painful or traumatic. The gift of forgetfulness.

But he couldn't forget Caroline quitting him. Such had caused him to go on a very wild ride. One he might never have alit except for fact that fate had stepped in. Caroline married and divorced, and then Sheldon had died leaving half of his legacy to Landon.

He stirred, legs aching to be stretched. The sky growing lighter by the minute. His lonely vigil over for now, without incident.

Landon smiled as the light came on in the kitchen. He got out of the little car and made his way to the house.

"Yes," he said aloud, making his way up the walk. "A cup of Caroline, ah—coffee would really hit the spot."

Inside, he leaned heavily on the counter as she left for work. Beyond fatigued, he dragged himself up the stairs and collapsed in her bed. Where he slept like the exhausted man he was.

Late in the afternoon, he woke to Sandy's stirring rendition of the Aretha Franklin tune, "Respect." Why did everyone seem to think they could sing that song and sound like the Queen of Soul? Landon wished he had a pair of earplugs.

Yet he felt unexpectedly refreshed. He hopped out of the bed and into the shower. He showered, dried his hair, and dressed in short order.

Bounding down the stairs two at a time, he nearly ran over the housekeeper. She was on her way up with an armload of clean towels. "Sorry," he said. "That was quite a little concert earlier."

"You know what the Good Book says," Sandy grinned, "'Make a joyful noise.'"

"I would definitely say you did that!" Landon rolled his eyes.

In retaliation, Sandy walloped him with a fluffy towel.

A few minutes later, he sent her home early and cooked Caroline's dinner himself.

Landon had to admit he wasn't much of a cook. So he improvised a dish based on canned ravioli and wilted lettuce from the fridge, throwing in a chopped stalk of celery for good measure.

Caroline arrived from work, overwhelmed by the "gourmet" meal Landon had waiting. His saving grace presented itself in the fine bottle of Cakebread 1979 that he'd pilfered from her cellar. She had always said it went well with everything.

After dinner they talked and cuddled on the couch.

"I have to ask you something," she said, knitting her brows.

He rubbed her arm. "What's troubling you, besides what should be?"

"I've been thinking a lot about the business and my father's vision for it," she said, sipping wine. "I just don't think he would approve of 'Sinful Secrets,' no matter how much money we make airing the show."

Landon narrowed his eyes. "I hate to admit it, but I think you're right. If I had known how much trouble this type of format could cause, I would've never done the show in the first place."

Caroline let out something like a muted cry of delight, then gave him great big kiss.

Before they knew it, the time had come for him to resume his vigil.

"Well, maybe nothing will happen tonight. Chief Inspector

King may come up with something shortly, so I can spend my nights inside the house, stretched out by you."

"Landon Shafer, you are so bad!"

"So bad I'm good. Right?"

Caroline shoved him toward the back door.

Chapter Eighteen

Finally, she had them right where she wanted them. Landon out of town and Caroline at home, alone, for the weekend.

Marita sat down at her kitchen table and quickly loaded the thirty-eight. She was feeling damned smug, too. By tomorrow morning she would have everything she ever wanted.

Nevertheless, she wasn't happy. Landon had told her he was in love with Caroline. Then the next morning Marita hadn't given the bitch a chance to fire her.

Marita wanted to get even. Though she fancied killing them both, she knew she could never kill Landon. She also knew without him, there would be no money. Besides, she loved him. Loved him enough to kill anyone who stood in her way of having him.

She knew he didn't really want to be with Caroline. She had seduced him—that bitch—then convinced him that was what he wanted. With Caroline out of the way, things would be totally different. Marita felt certain of it.

Close to three in the morning, Marita's 1969 Volkswagen Beetle moved over the darkened streets. A plain, unbroken gray sky shaded the black trees. She rolled her window down to allow cool air inside. Dew saturated the grass and the temperature was about forty degrees. In the distance, the faint spritzing of a computerized sprinkler programmed to water before dawn, clicked to its distinct beat.

On Lake Shore Drive, she saw no other cars. The closer she came to the house, the faster she drove with the gun under the driver's seat. Less than three minutes later, she parked in an alley, one street over from her target destination.

Marita was determined to be in and out in less than ten minutes, barring any neighbors out walking their dogs, or doing some other blasted thing that might cause her delay.

With the revolver in her gloved hands, she headed for the house. Marita ran in several directions, her eyes darting about as she checked to see if anyone or anything was taking notice of her.

⟶✖⟨✦⟩✖⟵

Landon had spotted the would-be killer the moment the beige Volkswagen Bug had turned onto Lake Shore Drive. Now he could see more clearly. Black shirt, black gloved hands, black ski mask.

Then he saw the gun.

Recognition struck an awful spark behind his eyes. By the time his mind registered what was about to happen, a sense of doom descended like a shroud. He had to do something. But what? Think, dammit, think!

Deciding he mustn't worry just yet about whether the intruder was Marita, he realized he had time to make a single call on his cell phone before he started toward Caroline house.

⟶✖⟨✦⟩✖⟵

The jangling of the telephone called Caroline awake. She reached over and grabbed the handset. "IImm—"

"Caroline! Christ, wake up!"

She flipped on her side and pushed hair away from her face. "Landon?"

"Yes. Listen to me. Whatever you do, don't turn on the

172

light. Get out of the bed. Now!"

She sat up. "What?"

"Dammit, don't argue with me! Don't say another word. Be quiet for once in you life! Just listen and do what I tell you. Someone is getting ready to break in your house, through your kitchen door. And whoever it is has a gun."

Caroline threw off covers and jumped from bed. "Now what?"

"Don't say another word! Just put your pillows under the covers so that it looks like you're still in bed. Then hang up the telephone and get in the closet until you hear my voice. Hurry! I'm on the way."

The line went dead.

Attempting to remain calm, Caroline hung up the telephone and arranged the pillows as Landon had ordered. Then she dove for the closet door, fumbling with the knob. She yanked it open and flew in, pulling the door closed behind her, to crouch in the dark on the floor, amid the clothes. She moaned with raw fear.

Someone was breaking in the kitchen door. *Rap. Rap.* As if a butt of a gun was being tapped lightly on glass. Two seconds went by. *Crunch*—the muffled sound of a breaking window. *Swoosh,* as if something was tossed aside, maybe into the bushes.

In her mind Caroline pictured a gun being shifted into the intruder's other hand, a hand that would not be the one to fire the weapon. Then an arm reaching through the now broken windowpane to unlock the kitchen door. *Click.* Slow squeak. She knew the back door was open.

Oh, God! I don't want to die!

Chit. Chit. Caroline could hear the slow footsteps moving over the tiled floor of the foyer. The living room was next, then the stairs. She wanted to scream, but that would only give her away. Besides, Landon had told her to stay quiet and to stay put until she heard his voice.

She needed a weapon. Why had she never bought herself a gun? Damn! Now what was she going to do?

Suddenly, one of her father's old sayings came to her. "If your gun isn't loaded, don't even go to the fight. And if it is loaded, make certain it's with laser bullets."

As it was, the most deadly thing she had available with which to defend herself? A wire hanger! Wasn't that just great? No doubt about it, she provided a sitting duck. Don't panic. Landon has a gun and he's on his way. He will get here in time.

Muffled footsteps came up the stairs. One-two-three-four. Only eleven more to go. She snatched a hanger off the rack, then quickly decided it would be of little use. She groped for a high-heel shoe instead.

Top of the stairs now, came the intruder, toward the bedroom. Only the hallway to go.

Caroline broke into a sweat.

She was cornered. She considered leaving the closet, but was afraid. It wouldn't take long to be found. There was nowhere to run, nowhere to hide, other than in this damned closet!

Her bedroom door creaked. Catlike footfalls sounded on the carpet.

Bathed in a mist of perspiration, Caroline tried to make her intakes of breath silent. Landon, please, please hurry—

She sucked in a breath, pressed a hand to her mouth to keep from crying aloud.

Caroline knew that even in the semidarkness of the moonlight that illuminated the room, the encroacher could clearly see where her head was assumed to be resting on the pillow, beneath the covers.

Let it look real—

No more footsteps—no movement at all. Then the cocking of a gun—

"I had him once, you know. But he probably never told you that, did he?"

Marita's voice. Certain of that, Caroline did not move.

"I could have had him again, forever this time. If only you had stayed out of his life. But, no. You had to have him—you had to have everything. The station and half your father's money weren't enough, were they? No. You had to have it all—You don't love Landon. I know it, even if he doesn't. No, you don't love him. I love him. You just love his half of the money. Well, I won't let you have it—I won't let you have him! And no one will ever prove I was the one who killed you."

It was a murder confession that sounded like a dime-store romance novel.

"Sit up, you bitch! I want you to see who's putting a bullet in your pretty brain!"

Still, Caroline did not move. She knew that any moment Marita would press the gun's barrel to where her head should be, and then realize the shape beneath the coverlet was not a head at all! What would happen next?

Oh, damn. I'm dead. I'm dead.

"Drop the gun, Marita," Landon said sharply. "Raise your hands in the air. Do it slowly."

Caroline stared at the closed door as if she were blind. As she took a breath and held it, the few seconds that passed seemed more like hours. Until finally Landon snatched open the closet door just in time for her to see Marita spin around to face him.

He yelled for Caroline to switch on the overhead light. When she did, she gasped at the sight of Marita with a gun and the blinking of her eyes, before they thinned behind the slits in the knitted mask.

Landon's gun was trained directly on the gunwoman. Caroline quickly moved to stand next to him. His face betrayed his open rage as he took a half step forward and maneuvered into a better position, keeping his gun pointed on Marita. He gripped the Beretta tighter.

For the first time, Marita seemed to focus on what happened around her. Her face in a spasm, she looked at Landon and Caroline. Then shook her head quickly.

"Don't do it, Marita," Landon said. "Do you hear me? Don't give me a reason. I don't want to shoot you, but if you give me cause, so help me, I'll shoot you down."

But Marita made no move to comply.

"Caroline," she said defiantly. "She is the one you should be pointing the gun at. Kill her and then we will be together and have everything. We were meant to be together—I love you! Kill her."

"You sick, miserable—This has nothing to do with her and everything to do with money. You want her dead so that you can have me, and her part of the station through me." He turned toward Caroline. "Call the police."

Her heart skipped one beat, before Caroline nodded and went for the phone.

"You son-of-a-bitch," Marita growled and fired.

"Caroline!" At that moment his heart seemed to stop.

With all the hatred and fear imaginable, with a speed he didn't know he possessed, Landon fired on Marita.

The bullet exploded somewhere in her upper chest and took her down with force. Immediately, she rolled flat on her stomach, shaking. Along with her arm, the revolver hit the floor.

He shot forward, grabbed it, and twisted the revolver from her unmoving hand.

Then she turned her masked head to the side and looked at him. He watched in horror as she closed her eyes and went still.

Breathing heavily, he turned back toward Caroline to see her slide down the wall, leaving a blood trail behind her on the off-white paint. Smoke and powder filled the air. He ran to her and went to his knees. She didn't move. She didn't open those huge blue eyes. She lay limp and quiet, but her blood ran beneath his hand. He felt her carotid arteries; there was a pulse. And she was breathing. Thank, God. He leaned forward and pressed his lips to her forehead.

Please don't die, Caroline. I need you. You are everything to me. You are my life. Please, don't die—

While keeping a cautious eye on Marita's motionless, prone body, he grabbed the telephone and dialed 911, and screamed as if he was talking through a child's handmade tin can and string walkie-talkie. "This is Landon Shafer. There has been a break-in and a shooting! Two shootings. Send an ambulance."

"Mr. Shafer, where are you?"

"The Hunt beach house on Lake Shore Drive!"

"Sir, you need to calm down. Is the intruder still there?"

"Caroline's been shot! Please hurry!" He dropped the phone then and focused on his beloved. When the initial shock wore off, fear hit Landon hard. Harder than anything he could have ever imagined.

Caroline can't be dead. Hurt maybe. Even badly. But not dead. No, not dead.

But she was slumped, almost sitting, with her back against the wall, her head hanging to one side. A small stream of blood ran from her forehead to her chin. He turned her face to the side and slipped his fingers under her jaw in order to get a better look at the head wound. From what he could tell, it looked to be more of a big gash than a penetration, but there was so much blood—and he was no damned doctor! He shook as if he had been the one shot instead of her.

"Come on. Come on, Caroline. Please wake up," he mumbled as he brushed her hair away from her bloody face. "Oh, baby, stay with me. Please, stay with me."

He watched the clock. It took ten minutes for the first police car to arrive, a second arriving soon after. Quickly another patrol car followed. Then an ambulance. When the sirens screeched they seemed to go on forever before Landon heard feet scrambling up the stairs. Yet another police car. Red and blue lights throbbing outside the window illuminated the night and began to attract a crowd. Then the police and paramedics appeared in the bedroom doorway.

As medical personnel rushed to stabilize Caroline for transport and to put her on a stretcher, Landon looked over at

Marita, lying in a pool of blood on the carpet.

Surely, I haven't killed her.

His head spun wildly with visions of red and blue lights. Suddenly he wanted Marita to live. He could deal with shooting her, because he had had no choice. But could he deal with killing a living person? Even a crazy one?

He didn't know. He didn't want to know.

He lost track of time as he followed Caroline on the stretcher out of the house and to the ambulance. The crowd outside seemed to enlarge by the second. As he jumped in the back of the ambulance for the ride to the hospital, the coroner's van arrived.

Landon knew Marita would not be coming to the hospital with them. She would go to the morgue.

Suddenly he felt nauseated and his skin became covered with perspiration. He left the ambulance and vomited behind some bushes. Twice. He wiped his mouth and got back inside.

As a paramedic adjusted Caroline's IV, Landon touched her cheek. "Will she be all right?"

"She has a nasty gash from that bullet on her forehead and a concussion but, yes, I think, barring any other complications—"

Caroline groaned. "Complications, my butt," she murmured and opened her eyes. "I'm too mean to die, Landon, and you know it."

Chapter Nineteen

As Caroline's senses gradually returned, distant voices came nearer until she realized that two sets of eyes were regarding her. Sandy and Landon stood on one side of her bed. The sight of them bending over her warmed her heart like nothing else in her life ever had.

But where was she?

A nurse dressed in a maroon tunic and white pants, no cap, came into her line of vision, giving Caroline the first clue. The second was the plastic name tag she wore that read "RN" after her name. Oh, yes. The hospital.

Then she remembered: Marita standing with a gun.

Marita had shot her—but she wasn't dead. In fact, she was very much alive.

Sandy spoke first. She looked tired, her gray eyes shadowed by bluish circles. "I'm so sorry this had to happen to you, Caroline."

Landon moved closer. "Are you awake?"

She blinked. "I guess so."

"I'll get a doctor," the nurse said.

Landon bent forward and stroked her hair. "I am so glad you're finally awake. I was beginning to worry about you."

"Just now you're beginning to worry about me?" Caroline licked her dry lips. She touched the bandage on her forehead and grimaced.

"You're in pain."

She lifted her head, but that made it begin to hurt more, so she closed her eyes. "Not too much anyway. Did Marita shoot me in the brain?"

Landon sighed heavily. "Almost. But, thank God, the bullet only grazed you. They're going to do some tests this afternoon to make certain you have no other damage. The doctor is pretty sure you don't though. Do you remember what happened?"

"Some." She gazed up at him. "We caught Marita trying to kill me. You held a gun on her while I went to dial for help. That's when—"

"That's when she shot you," he said.

"And then—?"

Landon touched her hand. "And then I shot her."

"Is she dead?" Caroline closed her eyes briefly and tried to visualize Landon killing anyone—She couldn't picture it.

"Yes," he said. "She's dead. Do you feel well enough to talk about it?"

Caroline nodded, then eased into a sitting position, and focused on the IV in her arm. Nausea and clamminess developed instantly along with the pounding inside her head from the sudden exertion. Waiting for the pain and nausea to subside, she gazed down at her body.

There was a short knock on the door and the nurse came back into the room. She handed Caroline a small paper cup. In it were two very large white pills.

Caroline scrunched up her nose. "I suppose you want me to take those?"

The nurse never answered, only said, "One is for pain and the other is an antibiotic." She poured a glass of water. "The doctor is making rounds right now. He will be here in a little while to check on you."

"Will he have smaller pills?"

"Swallow," the nurse said.

Caroline obeyed, although not without showing her displeasure by making a face.

She looked up at Landon, making no effort to conceal the desire for him that had sunk so deeply into her through the years that she no more noticed it than she noticed the rising sun of each new day. No matter all he had been through in his life, and recently with her, his only concern was for her. She'd been selfish. She had kept her need from him even more carefully than she'd kept it from herself. No more.

She'd waited a lifetime to love Landon and she would not waste another moment repaying him for what he had given her. With his love, he had given her life. With her love, she would show him every day how special he was.

"Caroline, are you all right?" he asked worriedly.

"Yes, fine. Why?"

The laughter that suddenly filled Landon's eyes turned them a beautiful chocolate brown. The slant of his cheekbones and his defined mouth were heightened rather than blurred by his smile. She was truly blessed to have him in her life.

"It just seemed like you were off in another world for a moment."

"Yes. No. That is—" Caroline's gaze searched Landon's face. "Not another world, only this world with you."

He reached and touched her hand. Suddenly she wondered what it would be like to look into the sleeping face of a baby and see hints of Landon's beloved face.

She said, "Finish telling me what happened after I went into never-never land."

He sat down next to her on the bed. "There's really not much else to tell you. After the shooting, Chief Inspector King went to search Marita's apartment and found her diary." He hesitated, his voice low and reluctant as he added, "Everything she did to you, and with me, was pretty much all detailed. Along with the plan to murder you while I was out of town."

Caroline gasped. "You're kidding. But, why would she want to leave such evidence lying around?" She shook her head. "It doesn't make sense."

Landon agreed and gripped her hand tightly in his. He fixed his dark gaze on hers and said solemnly, "No, it doesn't. At least not to a normal person it doesn't. But when I asked one of the inspectors that exact same question, he said if these kinds of people never get caught, they can never be famous."

"Unbelievable. So he was saying Marita wanted to get caught. Just for the notoriety it would bring her?"

"Apparently." Landon shrugged. "I guess any attention is better than no attention to people in her disturbed state of mind."

"That's so sad."

Eyes fixed on Caroline, he said, "And I think you're being overly generous. The woman tried to kill you, remember?"

"Don't remind me."

Then Landon said, "Oh, I almost forgot. The only thing found on the doll that could be tested was a single strand of hair. The good news is, this morning the DNA results from the test run at the lab showed that it was an exact match to the blood smear Marita had left on the chair arm, in Chief Inspector King's office."

Caroline laughed and it hurt. "The results came back?"

"Yeah. A tad bit after the fact. But the evidence does serve to put a lid on the case permanently."

She nodded.

"I'll remember this day until the day I die," Landon said.

And I'll love you until the day I die.

Feeling safe, surrounded by people who cared about her and wanted her to get well, Caroline closed her eyes.

And slept peacefully.

Chapter Twenty

Sunrise at Miller Beach was always spectacular. It flamed on the eastern side of the island. Just like the afterglow of their always cataclysmic lovemaking, Caroline thought as she rested after Landon had left for the police station to make one last official statement downtown.

Something in his eyes made her want to lose herself in his arms. If Landon only knew how lonely her life had been before now, how long she had felt so alone. If he knew how badly she'd wanted someone to come along and change her life, someone to give her back her heart, he would understand.

In his arms, it felt like home to her. Finally, she felt as if she were on her way back to where she belonged.

The jangling of the telephone caught her attention.

She stretched like a cat. "Mmm—Hello?"

"Happy, happy birthday, baby," he sang, a little off-key. Then said, "Have I told you lately that I love you?"

Rolling on her side in bed, she smiled. How sweet that he'd thought to call her from the police station just to say happy birthday. Especially after everything they had just been through.

"Landon, you have never told me you loved me," she said.

"Then don't you think it's about time?"

"I think so. It would be nice to hear it."

"Caroline, I've got something I need to do. Can you hold on a minute?"

"I guess so."

She hoped he wouldn't need to stay downtown much

longer. He'd already been there a good hour and a half. After just being released from the hospital, she had no desire to be alone any longer that necessary.

"Good morning, Miller Beach!" Landon's voice boomed over the wire. Caroline snatched the receiver away from her ear and stared at it as if it had two heads. Returning it, she heard:

"This is Saturday, February fourteenth, and this is a Valentine's Day special edition of the Magic 97 'Morning Show.'"

Caroline jackknifed to flip her radio on. *He wouldn't have really called me on the air—would he?*

"You're on the air with John and Melissa and, yours truly—The Love Doctor, Landon Shafer—this morning's Morning Crew."

She guessed so—

At that moment a high-pitched shrieking sound came through the radio's speaker. Over the phone, "Ma'am, could you please turn your radio down?"

Caroline almost fell off the bed, reaching over to lower the volume. Quickly she focused all her attention back on the voice coming through the receiver of the telephone:

"This is Valentine's Day, finally. Ten minutes past seven with The Morning Crew on this Lover's Day. Any news, Melissa?"

"You bet, guys. News this hour is that women are crying all over the world this morning."

Landon must have moved his receiver in front of Melissa as she spoke.

"Why's that?"

Caroline recognized John's voice in that question.

"Well, John," Melissa said. "Our very own Love Doctor is no longer the most eligible bachelor on the East Coast of Georgia."

"You're kidding! You mean us regular guys finally have a chance with the ladies around here? Even the ones that don't shave their chest?"

"Looks that way," Melissa said. "Says here, Landon Shafer is in love with Caroline Hunt."

Caroline choked. If she hadn't already been sitting, she would have fallen down.

"Are you sure?" John asked.

"Well, Landon is right here with us," Melissa said. "Why don't you ask him yourself?"

"Good idea, Melissa. Landon—is it true you love Caroline?"

"More than life itself, John. Caroline, are you still on the line?"

"Yes. I'm here." She could barely speak for the tears in her throat.

"Will you marry me?"

"Will I marry you?"

"Yes, my sweet, sweet, Caroline. Will you marry me?"

She wiped her eyes with a corner of the sheet. "Yes, I will marry you!"

"Should I meet you at home?"

"Please do, darling. Just don't take too long—"

"I wouldn't think of it."

"Oh, Landon?"

"Yes?"

"One more thing."

"Anything for you."

"You are the sun in my sky, Landon. Love me as much as I love you. I need to hear you say you love me."

"I love you!"

No longer would she ever deny herself or Landon Shafer—not anything! It was at that moment Caroline Hunt knew her dreams would be forever sweet, until death they did part.

Genesis Press titles are distributed to the trade by
Carol Publishing Group
120 Enterprise Avenue
Secaucus, NJ 07094
1-800-447-BOOK (Phone)
1-800-866-1966 (Fax)

Genesis
Press

315 3rd Avenue North
Columbus, MS 39701
Tel: (601) 329-9927
Fax: (601) 329-9399
http://www.genesis-press.com